EQUATORIAL
RHYTHMS

EQUATORIAL RHYTHMS

ROBERT A KAMAROWSKI
MOUNTAIN ASH PRESS

to tom, kornel, kris and samantha.

true friends. thank you.

yea, slimy things did crawl with legs
upon the slimy sea

samuel taylor coleridge
the rime of the ancient mariner

sea devil

one

the line is tossed into the air   it traces a wide arc in the
sky   twisting like a snake   floating in a strange world
that's all light and movement but without a voice   a gull
floats by against the cloudless blue   cars pass silently on a
distant bridge   a church steeple stabs its pointed spire into
the cool air   a thin shadow moves across the filthy
water   the line strikes its head against the white hull   and
the silence is broken

we haul like demons   muscles straining against dress
whites   fingers gripping the line   arms and backs pulling
as one   brothers in our labor   a giant hand condemned to
perform one task   haul and haul and haul   i'm in some kind
of trance   everything is blurry   out of focus   feeling only
the thick rope against my skin   until the eye whips through
the chock like the head of a snake   i jump forward and play
the rope out neatly against the gray deck   putting it to rest

i move to the lifeline and take my place next to the rest of the
crew

        all hands attention on deck!

we're all lined up   stiff as pilings   a band plays on the
pier   family and friends wave   a woman holds a white
handkerchief to her face   a father salutes his son   and the
tug churns the murky water into mad yellow foam as it drags
the owasso into the center of the thames   the ship's horn
shatters the sky   the engines grind to life

we leave new london behind   set sail for rio   and the
equator

two

i lie in my rack   the ship rocks me back and forth   i'm an
infant   a baby to the world   my stomach is adjusting to
the sea   my head to my stomach   laughter   obscenities
slamming locker doors   the noises of the pit   the sounds
crawl along the exposed pipes and ladders and blue peeling
paint and the chipped green tile deck   not trying to escape
but looking for me   the swirling sounds like a drug   a
ticking watch swinging slowly back and forth

my eyes are closing

music   a guitar   the strings sending gentle notes into my
head   a voice sings off-key   i climb out of my rack   the
rolling ship is fogging my head   placing a gray mist in front
of my eyes   tugging at my legs   trying to knock me off
balance   i peel off my pants and shirt and hang them on
the chain that holds up my rack   i climb back onto the thin
mattress that sits on a piece of canvas   more voices   more
laughter   more music   more swearing

visions in my head   jennifer   a baseball game   an album
i bought before i left   a long drive down route
two   jennifer's breasts   a film of sweat highlighting her
skin   the moon lighting up the branches of a tree in
silver   the ocean below   the sky above

sleep

a hand shakes me   kelly's voice

```
     you gonna eat rat
```

the fog in my head is still thick

```
     rat!  hey!  you gonna eat
```

```
     no no     later
```

he leaves me   i stare at the canvas above   i want to get back
to the dream   there was black everywhere
deep   unending   and a woman   not a girl   a
woman   like a movie star   black hair   black dress   lots
of curves   long legs   green eyes   she licks her red
lips   she reaches out for me   she wants me   i close my
eyes   but she's gone

three

kelly's voice again

    `yo rat    hey slick you ehva gonna eat`

my head clears this time   my stomach is steady

    `yeah yeah    wait for me kelly`

i blink   run a hand over my bristly head   sit on the edge of
my rack ducking under the canvas above   my foot hits
something below

    `rat    whatthefuck huh`

    `sorry speed    sorry       hey speed    you`
    `goin' for breakfast`

    `no man    i'm sleepin'    whatthefuck huh`

i dress and follow kelly   up two sets of ladders   down
narrow passageways with green bulkheads rising on either

side   rivets sticking out like stitches over a series of
wounds   the scars running up and down the ship in neat
rows   the cuts made with something specific in mind   not
done in a fight   but by a surgeon

the ship is riding nice and smooth not rocking really just a
gentle roll from port to starboard   settling into the sea like
easing yourself into a fat cushiony chair   getting
comfortable getting ready to spend some time there

the chow line is halfway up the ladder   i rub the sleep from
my eyes   we inch our way down   kelly's silent   he knows
it takes me time to wake up   especially when we first set sail
   when i'm fighting the rolling of the ship   the movement of
the sea   in the galley   we each grab a tray and move
down the line   the chow's some kind of meat or something
 it's turned to liquid   or maybe it's gravy and the lumps are
supposed to be meat   the mashed potatoes look green   the
vegetables a little pale   like things have switched colors   i
grab extra bread to stuff myself

we find an empty table

        the galley's packed

kelly looks around

        the cadets   don't fawget that's why
        we're here

```
yeah    that's why we're goin to rio
instead of just sittin out in the middle
of the ocean


and why weeah just day woorkas this
trip        no watches      gonna be like a
cruise rat


are these boys close to being officers


i'm not shooah
```

ericson sits at our table   grumpy as usual   he's a skinny guy
like me   but he has these cheeks that look stuffed with
food   and he always has this three day old beard   an hour
or two after inspection it's like it magically grows to give his
face this scruffy look   he puts his plate down and starts
eating without saying a word   kelly looks at me and smiles

```
mawnin ericson


good morning to you kelly            rat
```

he chews his food a while   swallows   takes a sip of coffee

```
whatta you think a these fuckers
```

he nods at a table of cadets next to us   three are eating very
slowly   like they're considering whether the food is safe or

not   a fourth's food sits untouched   his chin rolls across his
chest eyes closed   i can tell he's fighting it trying to stop the
world from rolling

ericson looks at the sick cadet

> ```
> hey puke    what the fuck   you don't like
> the food    hey   yo   puke   maybe you
> need a little tabasco sauce on that meat
> ```

the cadet looks up   he stares at the person across the table
from him like he's in a dream   then he puts his hand over his
mouth and stumbles out of his seat and races for the head

the regular crew laughs   some make noises like they're
throwing up

ericson looks at us

> ```
> my last time      my last time out and i
> have these fuckers with me           this
> is going to be a blast
> ```

and he returns to his food

sailors are scattered over the fantail flesh colored bumps
against the gray deck like acne on an old face   without
shirts   suntan lotion making the skin shiny as if its
wrapped in some type of clear plastic coating   it's
sunday   holiday time   do what you like   even a few of the
snipes are up here   their skin pale as a ghost from the lack of
sun   they creep up from the engine room and sit in
groups   oil stained hands filthy pants and boots   like
they're a different species   like they're from another
world   they talk real loud they laugh real loud and their
conversation always seems to drift eventually to engines
 ships or cars it doesn't really matter   like they're unable to
direct their minds toward any other subject except maybe
women

kelly and i sit on the fantail   he reads a book or should i say
devours it   his eyes racing across the pages eyebrows
bunched together oblivious to the world around him   his
appetite for reading's like an obsession it's a difficult job
finding him without a book   he always has one in his back
pocket   i've tried to develop the habit myself   once i pick

up a book and open it and begin to read the pages i get lost in
another world   as though i'm not even on the ship any
more   but it's difficult for me to open that first page   i sit
and think all the time   wonder if my time in the coast guard
will ever be up   wonder what i'll do on the outside when i'm
finally out   wonder if i'll go to college like i said in all my
letters or if i'm just wishing out loud as if that will make my
time go faster   i wonder how lonely my mother is without
my father wonder if she really is lonely   i wonder why
jennifer broke up with me

kelly sips his coffee   he's always drinking the stuff
black   a little sugar   says it keeps him regular   says he's
going to get a lifer's hooked finger if he's not careful   his
slender face is soft and hard   like it's made of clay   shaped
by powerful fingers   with a little boy smile

the sea rolls away in giant mounds of blue and green like
moving hilltops   it makes me feel not quite real   like i'm
not really me   am i moving away from these liquid
hills   or are they travelling away from me   making a long
slow journey around the earth and some day will return to
this spot and another sailor will see them   or i'll be at a place
on the ocean where they'll happen to be passing by and i'll
see them again

a gull flies out over the transom   the new guy holmes tosses a
piece of bread up over the side   the bird dives and grabs the
bread and then returns to the transom as if it's some weird

kite being flown from the back of the ship on an invisible
line   holmes tosses his last piece of bread into the air and
then hangs his head   he puts his hands in his pockets and
walks back into the ship

kelly watches him disappear

```
remembah yowah first trip out to
sea       i remembah mine like it was
yestady    i thought i was a real sailah
till then   comin from new bedfud 'n
all      i was so lonely i couldn't
stand it
```

i try to forget those days   the loneliness   the overpowering
seasickness   days spent staring at the rack over my head
wondering how i got into this mess   praying for my last day
in the coast guard to come out of the night and take me home
  take me away from all these different people with their
different ideas and different sense of humor and their lack of
concern for my sickness   even making fun of me   laughing
at me to my face

```
i remembah being so lonely   until hump
day   and you and i were washing the
gahbage off of us in the showah   and we
started to laugh about it      remembah
```

he smiles out over the sea

```
that was one of the best moments of my
life     and it helped me get through this
whole coast gahd thing      i'm almost at
home heeah now
```

kelly takes a sip of coffee   he gets a few grounds and makes
a face at the bottom of his cup   he walks over to the lifeline
and tosses the rest of it into the sea   feet spread apart he
stands and watches the rolling ocean   but i turn and
watch the gull sway from side to side on his invisible line
waiting for more bread

five

stars hover in the sky   as though they're filled with helium
and have climbed into the night until they can't go any higher
and now just watch the earth below   the moon's a thin strip
of curved silver   an ornament   hung from an invisible
branch   the engines rumble underneath me   a warm
breeze plays against my skin   rowdy voices invade the night
and then fade into the darkness with the slam of a hatch   the
world's so big   and so small   sea and sky   endless rolling
black   it's an ocean stretched out forever   beyond my
eyes   beyond my head   wrapping itself around the earth
like a cold liquid skin   and yet without land its sameness
makes it so small   like looking through the fisheye lens of a
camera with all the boundaries easily visible   a distorted
blue sphere   a peep hole through which i can see half the
earth at once   and if i look hard enough maybe i could see all
the land and all the people just along the edge   almost in
sight but not quite   tiny and insignificant   toys in a toy
land   i feel I could shake the earth and watch the false snow
slowly tumble to the ground

```
                        six
```

the hole

leblanc lies back on huge sacks filled with rags   his thick
body looks as if it's in a giant chair   ericson cleans his
fingernails with the point of a knife   kelly reads a tiny
paperback with his wire rimmed glasses sitting halfway
down his nose   gomez twists and folds the pages out of
an old magazine   his fingers move so fast it's like a strange
dance   i have no idea what he's making but i know it'll be
interesting   speed half sings half hums a slow song   his
voice high and clean and sharp   holmes sits in a corner
staring at the ends of his fingers   afraid to look up
   especially afraid to meet ericson's eyes   wanting to avoid
more abuse   as if not making eye contact could spare him
from ericson's tongue

steps on the ladder   heavy   thudding   the sound of feet not
used to moving about the ship   three cadets peer through
the cage   their eyes moving over our forms like we're rare
animals in a zoo

is this the boatswain's hole

leblanc doesn't even open his eyes

fuckin' ay ace

they enter the hole and nod at us   waiting for some type of
greeting   innocently standing there and expecting a
warm reception   maybe a sign that we're glad to see them or
something   or maybe that they're welcome here   one is the
cadet who got sick in the galley

ericson looks up from his manicure and takes note

hey puke   how you doin'   you try that
tabasco sauce yet or what

he shakes his head

fuckin' pukes

more steps on the ladder   this time they belong to chief
wheeler   he bends his slender form under the
entrance   thinning hair slicked forward as if he's fooling
someone as if the world can't see he's going bald   his lips
are pressed together turning them a little white   like he's
mad or thinking real hard   he's a nice enough guy I guess
 just putting in his time   counting days until he
retires   pretty knowledgeable   a pretty good teacher
  but a disappointment to most of the deckies   they like to

cut themselves out as a rugged bunch   maybe even a little
mean   and they want a chief who comes off that way   like
a gang leader   but that isn't chief wheeler

he looks at the cadets and nods

```
i'm chief wheeler    i guess you'll be
working with us for most of the trip
i'll assign you to one of my men here the
first few days    just until you get the
hang of things    and then you're on your
own
```

they nod   i can see they're still waiting for more   these are
the men of the academy   these are the future officers of the
coast guard   these are the future captains of ships   they
probably spend twenty-four hours a day being told how
special they are   how tough they are   how only a few can do
what they're doing   and even chief wheeler isn't giving
them a decent greeting   it's funny   i wonder how they'll
view deck hands when they're done here   i guess we're
reinforcing their feelings that we're uneducated uncouth low
life human beings whose lack of ambition has led us to be
deck hands on a coast guard cutter   and maybe they're
right

the chief refers to his little green book

```
ericson    take holmes    hook up a
boatswain's chair under the starboard
```

```
bridge wing and finish painting there

hey hey hey     it's you and me
holmes        you're gonna love this
common boot

kelly and speed     continue working on
the stanchions on the port side
```

a tripping of footsteps on the ladder and rodgez enters the hole   red hair sticking out of his cap at insane angles   like spikes of fire   red mustache and eyebrows mixing with the freckled face   his short bowlegs carry him over to the workbench

```
sah sah sah sorry chief     no body
wowowowoke me up   heh heh
```

the chief frowns and looks back at his book

```
rat   take the new men and get them going
on the fantail     all those chocks and
bits need to be painted     show them
where to get the paint     and what kind
to use
```

i grab some rags and hand one to each cadet

```
follow me
```

seven

they're nice enough guys I guess   not giving me a hard time
accepting the fact that they have to do deck work manual
labor get their hands dirty   they paint under the sun with
bare backs shining   casting squat dwarfish shadows on the
deck   the one cadet got sick again   we were at the bow of
the ship in the paint locker where the pitching of the ship's
exaggerated   like being on a carnival ride that rises and falls
and rises and falls   fumes from the paint and thinner and
turpentine and rags soaked with all of it blow a disgusting
wind when you first open the hatch   i got sick myself there
once   the cadet held off as long as he could   i watched
him go white as the ship   it was funny really but I didn't
laugh in front of him   he placed a hand on his stomach and
one over his mouth and raced for the head   to my surprise it
was the other cadets who laughed out loud   they made
remarks about his weak stomach   one even called him
puke   i just listened and smiled   and i don't think this was
for my benefit they really wanted to dump on this guy but
the more they talked the more i had the feeling they were
jealous of him   'mr perfect' they kept calling him   'mr
know-it-all'   they were happy he was getting sick on a
regular basis

the three of them work steadily now   not hard but enough
to be getting something done   the guy who keeps puking
looks a lot better   harvey   he's working harder than the
other two   trying to make up for getting sea sick maybe or
trying to be one of the guys   he probably knows he's
different   yeah   he's definitely working harder than the
other two

     you guys doin' okay

     we're fine

     i'm goin' for a little walk around deck
     you run out of paint you know where to get
     more   you can find your way back to
     the paint locker   right

     no problem rat

rat   hearing him say my name is odd   not like an officer but
like a deckie   just another working guy just another
average joe   sorry sport but you're not   i'm a deckie and
someday you're gonna be an officer and maybe even make
my life miserable   maybe jump all over my case for some
petty nonsense or maybe come in hung over and make us
strip and paint something we stripped and painted the
previous day   maybe make some remarks right to my face
about people with no motivation no skills   no ambition
   have a good trip   and pretend all you want   but you're
no deckie

eight

i stroll along the deck occasionally leaning against the
lifelines and looking out over the long rolling waves   speed
and kelly are doing a little painting and a lot of
jawing   speed talks real fast   spit firing words like they're
bullets out of a machine gun   and sometimes mixed with
'dadadada' or 'eheheheh' which makes it seem even faster
  he's got kelly laughing about something and he won't let
up   he's talking faster and faster and kelly's laughing harder
and harder   i'll be surprised if they get three stanchions done
today   kelly holds his side while speed is leaning over
him   his face pointing down like a gun at a target   they
get three stanchions done this trip it'll be a minor miracle

i pass the bow of the ship   check a few lines   make sure no
rust is coming through the paint on deck and then move
around to the port side where ericson is staring up under the
bridge wing

        what the fuck boot   you gonna do some
        work today or what the fuck huh

he turns his gaze toward me and raises his hand in a sign of
frustration

        boots rat   fuckin' boots

he looks above him again

        you gonna do anything today or just sit up
        there and jerk off   huh   hey
        boot   huh

he shakes his head and walks away

up under the bridge wing holmes sits on a boatswains
chair   i can see his fingers are white where he's gripping
the line   in the other hand is a paint brush that hasn't been
used   the ship rolls gently to port and holmes and the
boatswains chair ride toward the bulkhead the ship rolls the
other way and he's dangling out over the ocean   his fingers
strangle the line

        yo   holmes   you okay

he looks down at me

        yeah   yeah   i guess

        just do it man   paint a little   hang on
        a little   just get it done sport

```
you gotta do this or he'll never let you
down

okay  okay        i'll do it

paint a little    hang on a little
you'll be done before you know it
```

he dips the brush in the paint can hanging from the
boatswain's chair and raises his arm above his head and dabs
a little paint before returning to his death grip

```
that's it holmes   a little at a time
```

he raises the brush and paints a little more

nine

the sun rests its chin on the sea   tired   preparing for
sleep   and thin clouds form a line across the horizon
cutting the sun at its forehead as rays of light burst from its
face blossoming into a huge cone   and way out in the
unknown something bleeds into the sky turning everything
scarlet

the sky changes to red like the lipstick painted on the woman
in my dream and streaks the ocean below with lines of blood

the cone of light becomes weaker and the sky turns pink

the sea lifts its chest to breathe once in a while   huge rolling
mounds of water that rotate the owasso

a gull flies across the sky   its black wings drift between the
clouds and the eyes of the sun seeking something   maybe
others of its own kind   it cruises in silence   the sun dips
its head beneath the horizon   only faint fingers of light
reaching for the sky

ten

the stars and moon are pasted in the sky and the ocean
occasionally twinkles with phosphorescence   lines slap
against the bulkhead   the wind flutters the open shirt
against my body   rubs its fingers across my face   a faint
noise comes from under the bridge wing   a whimper   like
an animal in fading pain   i walk slowly toward the noise
until a weak flashlight reveals a form hunched over
swinging slowly   its shoulders tremble as if chilled by the
warm night and i can hear crying   there is a moment of
calm   heavy breathing   an attempt at self control
    and then the chest deflates pushing out a mournful sob

my feet scrape the deck

the figure jerks up

holmes looks down at me   silver streams slip down his
cheeks   his mouth is set in such a deep frown i wonder if it'll
ever smile again   his bright blue eyes are just tiny black
holes lost in the night now   he runs a sleeve across his
mouth and nose and his lips curl back   his voice fights
through

`fuck you rat!       just fuck you!`

two quick breaths enter his body like an attack   like forcing
its way into him   causing his chest to rise and fall   his eyes to
close even more   just tiny slits now as if opening them
completely will let more of the evil that hounds him enter his
body   his lower lip protrudes from his face   almost
grotesque in its size

and the sobs thunder out of his body

eleven

chief wheeler looks at his green book before he goes down to the hole flipping pages   i've been waiting for him

    how's it goin' chief

he looks up   a little startled

    hey rat   okay   i'm doin' okay   time
    to work

    chief   you got a second

    what's up rat

    listen uhhh   ericson's been pretty hard
    on holmes lately   maybe they
    shouldn't work with each other for a
    couple days

    hey   come on rat   ericson's hard on
    everyone   he even gave you the time

```
of your life when you first came aboard
remember
```

i look down the ladder   snapshot images of ericson's mouth
look back at me   like something living on its own   not
needing a body   and working all the time   never
resting   never sleeping   a constant stream of abuse
pouring out   directed at me   personal   deep   humiliating
 and him loving it   always with that smirk on his face

```
yeah     well     not everyone handles it
the same     you know what i mean

holmes'll be all right rat     he needs to
take his lumps like everyone else
```

chief wheeler moves down the ladder   i watch his back as he
goes   the crook in his step from a bad hip   the floppy ears
sticking out from his cap   can't he see what's happening
 or doesn't he give a shit

i follow him down to the hole

twelve

the chief calls out the work schedule   the cadets seem a
little more comfortable today   a little more cocky   they've
lost that wide eyed look   they've gotten over the fact we
don't give a shit about them   playing it cool
now   they grab a bunch of rags and head for the paint
locker   speed and kelly leave right after them   ericson
climbs up the ladder followed by holmes who stops and looks
at me for an instant   his eyes look tired   older   but his
expression gives nothing away   i can't tell if he's recovered
from last night   i can't tell if he's figured out that he needs to
deal with ericson's shit or go crazy   there's nothing in his
face that tells me one way or the other   he turns and
disappears

chief wheeler makes notes in his little green book   like he's
practicing to be an accountant when he gets out   or a
newspaper reporter   always jotting down notes and
messages   always referring to his little fucking book as if he
can't keep the smallest thought in his head   him and his
blooming best seller   i wonder what would happen if it was
lost or stolen i wonder what he'd do   maybe go nuts   have

us all strip searched and confined to quarters   or lined up
and shot for the crime of the century   or maybe he'd go into
some kind of depression   moping around all day
   rudderless   i can see him with his head down   shuffling
instead of walking   mumbling to himself   or maybe i'd
find him on deck some night   with the stars and moon
shining white in the sky   the waves rocking the ship gently
to sleep   crying his eyes out

thirteen

i move some lines across the hole   stow some tools
away   pile some rags in a corner more out of sight than
really being neat   chief wheeler goes up the ladder   rodgez
looks up after him a few seconds and then turns to me

```
hey ra ra rat      check thi thi thi
thiiiiiiiiis out huh
```

he pulls a flare gun out from under a bench and places it in a
vice

```
i'm trying to converververververt this
into a regulllllar gun
```

he tightens the vise and walks around the pistol   wiping at
the barrel   blowing dust off it   his bowlegs go in opposite
directions but somehow cancel each other out and move him
in a straight line   his squat body rotates with each step
   there's a carpet of thick red hair on his arms and sticking out
of his shirt   like fur   like a stuffed animal with a round face
that always has a little smile on it   he's one of those guys it's
impossible to get mad at   or at least stay mad at   and maybe

the one true sailor on board   portuguese   from new bedford
a lobsterman   says he was born on a boat   from a
family of eight or nine but i think a couple of the kids died
pretty young   he knows everything about lines and knots
and how to use a marlinspike without ripping his fingers
apart   never seen him even close to sea sick   worst weather
in the world with everyone white and trying not to vomit and
rodgez is walking around with a pickle and mayonnaise
sandwich wondering what's wrong with everyone   crazy
little guy

```
     and you are about to wi wi wiwiwiwitness
     the initial firrrrring       heh heh
```

he cocks the hammer and loads a round into the backside of
the pistol   he checks the alignment and then looks at the
gun from every angle imaginable   his red hair sticks out of
his cap like tiny wings   i think he'll fly away one day   get
caught in a stiff breeze and be lifted off the deck and out over
the sea   he ties a string to the trigger   pays out the line as
he walks behind a stack of boxes and hawsers   i follow him

```
     it's only a blan   blan blank      buuuuut no
     sense in taking any cha chachachachances
     heh heh
```

we squat behind the barricade   rodgez the little boy   huge
smile   skin turning red from ear to ear   he takes a
deep breath and closes his eyes and pulls the string

a muffled explosion

    `liiiiitle tooooo much powdah    heh heh`

we peer up and over at the pistol   the back end has been
blown completely off   it may be impaled in the bulkhead
somewhere   gray smoke circles the hole like dirty fog   a
small part of the handle dangles a moment and then falls to
the deck

we sit back down with our backs to the boxes

rodgez looks at me

    `neneneneneneneeeeeeds a little`
    `work              heh heh`

fourteen

it's like spring fever has touched the crew   everyone seems
to be whistling or laughing   lots of conversation on
deck   hands waving in the air eyes wide   even holmes
managed to smile at some raunchy joke a snipe told at
breakfast   the cadets are painting more or less on the fantail
  at least they start painting when someone comes into view
   i walk over to the port side and lean against the lifelines
and watch the mammoth sea roll powerfully along   a
flying fish dashes across the water as if being chased and then
plunges back into the sea   some puffy white clouds look as
though they're lost   and a gull at the fantail waits for more
scraps to be tossed overboard

jennifer elbows her way into my head   her long blonde hair
parted down the middle   sleeveless shirt hanging loose on
her body the outline of her nipples pointing at me   soft lips
no lipstick   natural   i wonder what she's doing now   is she
in her room   lying on her back staring up at the ceiling   or
out with friends   or by the river painting   or shopping for a
dress   something to wear on saturday night   something to
turn a few heads   i wonder who she's with

a hatch bursts open behind me   gomez leaps onto the deck
with an old rag tied around his waist like some sort of
skirt   he rotates his hips and makes waving motions with his
arms like a hula dancer   he starts to sing 'i want to live in
amayreeka' 'i want to live in amayreeka'   leblanc comes out
after him   different color skirt or rag i mean   he starts
dancing next to gomez and jumps in with the singing

   kelly!   same kind of rag skirt   his hips need a jump start
or something though   speed comes out after him and
tosses an old rag at me and joins the chorus line   kelly's
laughing and can't dance or wave his arms for shit i wrap the
rag around my waist tying it with just a bunch of loops and
twists and jump in next to speed   'i want to live in
amayreeka' 'i want to live in amayreeka' i try to follow
speed's lead   this hip thing is kinda weird but i'm hanging in
there with the arm wave letting my hands just kind of flap
around   boneless   speed can really sing and is getting
into it now   his voice rising and rising and melting into the
air   we start this movement where we stomp real hard on
the deck when we say 'a-MAY-ree-ka' and it actually sounds
pretty good   at least from where i am   we do four or five
choruses   really getting the beat down and even finding a
little rhythm with my hips   chief wheeler walks around the
corner   he stops and looks at us   his cap comes off and he
runs a hand through the few strands of hair left on his skull

   he moves his head slowly from side to side   i guess he'll be
writing in his little green book all night with this one   he
starts to smile but his gaze is pulled up to the bridge wing for
a moment   he turns back to us

```
okay      okay guys     lets go     back to
work      come on    come on    back to work
```

he claps his hands together and then moves slowly on   i look
up at the bridge wing and the old man's gaze bores a hole into
my head   he has that same expression on his face   i guess
you'd call it passive but with the lips turned down
slightly   as if he's smelled something bad but doesn't want
to make a big deal out of it   or maybe disgusted by the fact
that he has to deal with deckies   lowlifes   his eyes drill
farther into me   reaching to the center of my chest   i finally
turn and go back to the fantail knowing the old man would
stare me down for the rest of the trip if i let him

fifteen

i pause on my way to the pit   the snipes' quarters is strangely
quiet   the opposite of someone screaming in a library but
the same effect   eerie   nothing but hushed sounds from
the night watch as they struggle for sleep   a snore here   a
groan there   a word i can't understand maybe a name   i
take a few steps down the ladder and see someone on his
knees   it looks like he's praying   then i see his body shaking
and realize he's doing some kind of work i move to a different
angle   the chaplain kneels before his locker with a scrub
brush in his hand   he rubs at the metal   i move a little more
get a better look at what he's doing   spring fever i guess
  boys will be boys   might be   might be someone out for a
laugh   might be someone has a gripe against the chaplain
  someone he tried to save a little too hard   salvage someone's
soul with a little too much push   he can do that he'll be
quiet for days   reading his bible   talking to himself   and
then someone will ask him a question or he'll see something
he doesn't like and then you can't shut the guy up   this is
good that isn't do this don't do that don't you know your
soul's in mortal danger!   he can really rub the wrong way
  so now he's on his knees trying to remove the sticker on his
locker that says 'JESUS SAVES' because underneath it
someone's written 'green stamps'

sixteen

the day room is packed with sailors   cramped into the few
available seats   cross-legged on the deck   i squeeze
through the doorway and grab the last spot next to kelly who
reads a book oblivious to the noise circling the room

        yo kelly

        hey slick   come ta see the movie   huh

        what is it

        spaghetti westan   i fahget the name
        yowah man clint eastwood ahm pretty shuah

        how can you read with all this noise

he looks around the room

        didn't even notice till you mentioned it

he smiles at me and then returns to his reading   the vocal
abuse continues from the restless crowd   a relentless
pounding on the english language   reducing it to one

syllable words   obscenities   incomplete sentences
   little more than the grunts of some low society
membership based on how crude you can get   the dues of a
special club   i do my part i guess   but i don't get carried
away   i try to stay a little civilized   not that i'm like wally or
anything   like i have this great vocabulary   but i'm aware
of the rules   speak with fancy words and prepare for
abuse   some get away with it   wally does   he's a school
teacher who's not on the trip   even makes fun of everyone
else's disgusting vocabulary   tells us we're just upright
animals   and not very bright ones   neanderthals without a
lot of hair   biological mutants   yeah   that's one of his
favorites   but he's an exception   everyone loves to hear him
when he's on a roll   drilling these words into our heads   like
ostentatious   i took an ostentatious shit this morning   saying
things that half the guys don't get and the other half need
about twenty minutes back at their rack to figure out   he's
treated like a possession   a mascot   the kind of thing people
pull out at parties and say look what we have and then place
it back into the closet   not that all these guys are idiots
   some know more about engines and radar and radio
communications than i'll ever even come close to
understanding   but some are not real educated   they feel
uncomfortable around big words   and i guess they're the
ones who lead the word game   top this   bet you never
heard this before   bet you never heard these words put
together before   'suck nuts' is one of my favorites   struck
me as the product of a really sick mind   ericson's real
proud of that one

equatorial rhythms

cigarette smoke circles the room sucking up the talk of sex
and work and home and more sex   creating a huge cloud of
gray floating trash

the projector unwillingly comes to life

the lights are turned off

seventeen

i skip down the ladder   i'm flyin' cause kelly's buyin'   i enter
the forward day room   just soda machines for me but a
gambling parlor for the usual crowd   a couple of snipes
  leblanc   two filipino stewards   they sit in a dirty fog of
smoke   ashtrays at each end of the table like burial grounds
filled to overflowing with the ends of charred
cigarettes   the filipinos chatter in their foreign
tongue   each with a huge stack of coins in front of him   the
two snipes have a little change   leblanc has only three coins
left as he reads his cards   oblivious to the constant chatter
that'll make sure he walks away empty handed tonight
  cards slap the table   smoke is blown from a mouth   a
hand scratches a two day old beard   it's like looking at a
movie or something staged   like they're performers   all they
need are cowboy outfits and a piano player   another card
hits the table   money's dropped on top of the original bets
    all these looks of concentration   like their lives are at
stake   furrowed brows   shifting eyes   more money's
added to the pile   cards are slapped down   a filipino smiles
and then he rakes the money in with his hands

equatorial rhythms

    maybe tomorrow   maybe the day after   eventually
leblanc will win   just enough to keep him coming back

i jump up the ladder with the two sodas in my hand and hear
leblanc's fading voice as he curses his bad luck

eighteen

the pit is completely black   the ship rocks under me
dipping from side to side   the giant cradle again   i tuck my
arm under the thin pillow and its frail innards collapse
against my head   the ship creaks and groans   the noises
crawl around my rack and then touch me   not attacking me
  just settling their weight   i feel like we're all in a womb
   a woman gives birth to us each morning and then
unwillingly accepts us back each night   lets us reenter her
body   protects us   doomed to repeat the process the next
day   and the next   the banged up hull is her skin   a
little paint like a little makeup   not hiding anything   just
making her look cheap   and feel worse   thinking of days
past when she was full of life   when she was unsinkable

there's a click of metal   a flame rises into the night   the
multi-colored light gathers its breath   stretches its body up
into the dark   a cigarette is placed into the flame   the
sailor's face is thin bands of flesh and flickering
shadows   cheeks suck in and the cigarette end glows bright
red   blue smoke rises on an invisible current of air

a dream pushes its way out of a head   blunt noises   barely
words   through his mouth and into the outside world
   purging himself of some memory   or the beginning of a
nightmare   the beginning of a never ending battle with the
demons in his head   some embarrassing moment   a past
mistake   trivial but not to him

someone touches himself i don't know why i feel
embarrassed hearing this   it's the only act of passion left in
the center of the sea   the objects of desire left far behind in
a place that's difficult to imagine anymore

there's a picture in my head   a series of photos like a slide
show   jennifer's head is down as she talks to me   the
part in her hair like a white trail cut through the center of a
forest perfectly straight   the next frame she's looking at me
   tears suspended on her cheeks protruding lower lip   and
in the next frame she's handing the ring back to me
   it's small now that i think of it it's kind of funny
   comical   it's so tiny   weak   underdeveloped   never
really had a chance   how could such a tiny diamond have
held us together for long   it conjured up dreams of a life
together   but i guess i know why she gives the ring back to
me   i can't see our lives together   my world is the next
moment   the next slice of time   a fraction of a second
   she wanted to talk about houses and china and babies   i
wanted to talk about my next ocean patrol   or which beach
we should go to that day   or which restaurant or which
movie to go to that night or which game was on tv   she

wanted to go for rides into different neighborhoods   i
wanted to have sex   i miss her   i think about her once in
a while   but it's just not as important as i thought it would
be   and the last frame slides into my head   the huge old
oak tree hanging its limbs toward the ground   the bicycle
against the garage   the weathered house with the red front
door   and jennifer's back as she walks away

nineteen

we move steadily toward the tropics   each day the sun rises
higher over our heads   its rays grow stronger   rising to a
boil   and each night grows warmer   the stars change
their angle to the earth   and life aboard ship finds a
rhythm   breakfast   work   coffee   work   lunch
 work   supper   a movie   or a card game   or a book   or
just staring out at the sea   finally sleep   and slowly the
cadets become a part of the crew   they're supposed to be
spread out in the pit   sprinkled among the deckies   but
they've managed to end up in a group in one corner in the pit

even the ship seems to groan less at night   accepting us as
her own   deciding we're not so bad after all

speed and kelly stop their painting on the port side for a
moment to watch some dolphins   i join them at the lifelines
as one jumps out of the sea   before it re-enters the water
another jumps and another   and another   their skin
reflects different colors like a moving rainbow   and their
faces with crazy grins   their eyes bright as they dance above
the water they race alongside the ship   speed has his

hat on backwards   a stripe of white paint runs across his
forehead   kelly wipes the glass of his wire-rims   his
cheeks curl around his smile

farther up the ship ericson leans over and watches the
dolphins too   his eyes fixed on the acrobatics   but his head
seems far away   counting the days 'til he's out   or
thinking about his alcoholic father   or thinking of ways to
make holmes' life more miserable   out here he has some
control   or at least control over a new guy who hasn't
learned to face up to him   maybe never will   ericson sucks
deeply on the last of his cigarette and then flicks it at the
dolphins   who continue to dance despite his foul mood

```
                    twenty
```

a rough hand pushes against my shoulder   trying to take
me away from the woman with the red lips   the deep red
lips   that grow larger and larger

   too close and too large for me to see her face now   and the
tiny pink tongue   barely visible   a shy animal in
hiding   and a voice zooming in on me   starting from far
off   then growing so large it fills my head

```
     rat     hey rat      get up
```

i look into a face   a mound of flesh   hazy around the
edges   it takes a moment   the chief

```
     hey rat come on      we've got to board a
     ship

     board a ship    chief    we're in the
     middle of the fucking ocean

     get up rat    i'll tell you when you get
     up      muster in the boatswains' hole
```

i work my legs out of the rack   my feet hit the deck and i'm
awake like magic   there's still a lot of snoring in the pit   but
i can hear some movement too   the rattle of a belt
buckle   the rustling of pants and shirts

  two racks over gomez gets dressed his eyes just slits his
mouth half open   i put my cap on and tuck my shirt in   at
the ladder i meet kelly and speed

        what's up guys

        beats me slick   chief didn't say a woord
        just mustah in the hole

we climb the ladder and make our way out on deck we walk
aft   gomez catches up by my side his eyes are open now

        what's this all about rat   i wuz
        sleeping like a fucking baby

        i don't know   chief didn't say much
        just that we had to board a ship and to
        meet him in the hole

        board a ship   we're in the middle of
        the fuckin ocean

we walk down the ladder   lights from the hole burn my
eyes   ericson and leblanc are already sitting around

 leblanc has his hat pulled over his eyes and is making like
he's asleep   we all stretch out in different parts of the
hole   trying to look nonchalant   like we don't give a
shit   i'm dying to know what's going on   but i play this
game of too cool to care

the sound of footsteps coming down the ladder   it's
rodgez   his shirt's outside his pants and his hat's on
sideways

> ```
> whawhawhawhaaaat a fuckin dream i was
> havin'          this bebebebetter be
> ggggggood
> ```

he tucks his shirt in and sits on a large pile of rags   we
watch each other   or look at our nails or tie knots in the end
of a spool of six thread   i get up and start pacing   i know it
makes everyone crazy and it's not helping me either   so i sit
back down and open an abused copy of the coast guard
handbook and look at the pages on knot tying   trying to
figure out why they put so many knots in it we never use

the engines below rise a note higher

ericson looks up from his nails

> ```
> they're kicking this baby into overdrive
> ```

leblanc doesn't even look up

```
      last time we stayed at full speed too long
      we ended up in dry dock for four weeks
```

more footsteps on the ladder   the chief comes into the hole
and leans against the doorway   he makes notes in his little
green book   he's real intent on what he's doing   strings it
out for a minute   maybe two before he looks at us

```
      there's a boat in distress      it's broken
      down not far from us      so we're going
      to board with a team of engineers and see
      if we can help
```

he looks at the green book and flips the pages

```
      there'll be two enginemen         speed
      you're coxswain        ericson   you and
      leblanc are in charge of getting the
      lifeboat ready          make sure it's
      topped off and has a first aid kit   get
      any help you might need      kelly rat
      rodgez        where the fuck is holmes
```

```
      he's not here yet
```

```
      i woke him up      when we're finished here
      make sure he gets the word         like i
      was saying      kelly rat rodgez and holmes
      will guide the snipes on board and stand
      watch        armed
```

he looks up from his book   stares around the hole   even
leblanc raises his cap

        the word from up top is they think this
        ship's running drugs   they're not
        sure   it's international waters
        nothing we can do anyway   but they're
        in distress and we have to render
        assistance

he looks around the room   kelly speaks

        chief   it's been a few yeeahs since some
        of us have even held a gun let alone
        fiahd one

        that's why you're up early   we're still
        about three hours from the ship   the
        rifles are being dusted off   you're
        going up on deck to take a few shots

everyone's tongues are stuck in their mouths   the chief
looks from one man to another getting off on this   all puffed
up   looking tough   but i noticed he doesn't have to board
this boat with us

        the ship didn't ask for help   a tanker
        going by spotted them and got the story
           i'm not sure this ship even wants us on
        board   but we're close   and they

```
were talked into letting us have a look at
their engine    i don't think there'll be
trouble    but we have to be ready
```

i watch him consult his little green book again   loving this
stuff a chance to be macho without being macho give
orders but not get dirty   the star of the chiefs' mess i'll
bet   even the snipe's chief must be playing second fiddle to
wheeler now   i watch him a moment longer   fingering
his book   making little marks

i have to hear him say it

```
chief      you going over on the lifeboat
too
```

```
no    no i'm not rat    i'll be standing
by coordinating things between the away
team and the bridge
```

he turns back to his little book

it's heavy   that's the first thing that strikes me   like how
does anyone carry this thing around and then have the
strength to fire it   everyone else has an m16   they're
small   like plastic toys   but this thing is right out of boot
camp   it weighs a ton   jenkins the gunners mate stands
next to rodgez   he explains something   points to a part of
the weapon   rodgez puts it to his shoulder and fires   short
quick bursts   rags floating on a lifesaver drift about twenty
five yards from the ship   some of the rags fly apart

rodgez looks up with a huge smile on his face   like he won a
war

jenkins goes over to kelly and starts telling him to 'ease the
trigger back' and 'hold your breath just before you fire' and all
this other zen type of stuff   i can tell kelly's uncomfortable
with the rifle   maybe even more than me   and he looks
weird with his granny glasses on and a book sticking out of
one back pocket and a red bandanna out of the other
   jenkins steps back

kelly fires a couple of times   water ripples to the right of the target

jenkins tells him to adjust to one side   kelly pushes his glasses up his nose   a burst of bullets perforates the water and then tears up the rags as though invisible hands are shredding them   kelly turns and lets out a big breath   he sets the gun down   wipes his glasses

jenkins walks up to me

```
sorry about the m1 rat    we're not
prepared for this type of thing       the
old man is pissed off like nobody's
business      i said if we get in a real
scrape we should just put the five inch
mount on the fuckers    if they still
don't listen blow them back to wherever
the fuck they come from        boy     that
did nothing for his mood at all      me
i think the old man hasn't been laid since
the turn of the century   but what the
fuck    he's the old man right
```

he loads a round in the chamber   checks the sights

```
you heard what i told the others     right
nice and easy            make love to the
fucking trigger    easy rat
```

i raise the gun to my shoulder   close one eye   aim right for
the heart of the pile of rags   start to squeeze the
trigger   real slow   like it's in slow motion   taking
forever   thinking i'll bore someone to death and not have to
shoot the fucker

the explosion goes off in my ear

it feels like my right shoulder flies out the other side of the
ship   i stagger backwards   one foot crazily behind the
other   jenkins catches me before i hit something and fall
over   i can hear speed and rodgez laughing

 i look over at them   kelly has a big shit-eating grin on his
face

```
did i hit it

tell you the truth rat    i didn't even see
the water splash
```

this time i reload the rifle   jenkins tells me to keep both eyes
open

 everything is all messed up now   my eyes are going in and
out of cross-eyed   i can still hear rodgez trying to hold back
his laugh   i swing the gun to the left   to the right   i don't
know what the fuck is going on   i pull the trigger   there's
a sound on the deck   rodgez has fallen onto his knees and is
holding his side   kelly is draped over the lifelines

```
how bout that time
```

maybe kelly's crying and not actually laughing at me

```
no no no       still nothing
```

```
i guess i'm giving these fish a hell
of run for their money today
though huh
```

i think rodgez is going to bust something inside   jenkins reloads the gun   looking weird with a grin   fuck 'em all   i put the gun to my shoulder   close both eyes   the explosion seems even louder this time

   i assume I've hit the fucking ocean at least   rodgez is having some kind of shit fit   kelly's sitting with his back to me shaking like he's freezing cold or something   jenkins has lost all control   i think the guy's gonna piss his pants if he doesn't watch out

```
i know   i know      you didn't even see a
ripple right      hey it's only one
bullet        maybe it's right in the
center of the rags and you just don't know
it
```

rodgez's pounding his feet on the deck   kelly's still crying or

equatorial rhythms

freezing or whatever   jenkins is wiping his face   i place the
gun down

    `had enough big guy`

and jenkins can't even speak to answer me

twenty two

there's a special feel to this morning   even a few snipes are
out on deck watching the show   all these deckies getting the
small boat ready to be dipped into the drink   lines coiled
turnbuckles checked   guns stacked neatly on
deck   rodgez is so excited i can't understand a thing he's
saying   stuttering every word   taking so long to say
something i find myself leaning forward   wanting to reach
down his throat and drag it out for him   but i'm caught up
in all this too   i can't really explain what this feeling is   but
my heart does a slow turn in my chest   like it's going to
explode but doesn't   just keeps pushing at the walls of my
body   a feeling of anticipation and sorrow at the same
time   happy and sad   a lot like the day we get back from
ocean patrol   looking forward to hitting land i want it so
much to touch the earth to see friends   but i also don't
want it   i want that feeling of not quite being there to last
longer   stretch out   stop time   stop the ship in the
middle of the thames and watch all those people on the dock
waving   family and friends calling out to sailors on
deck   i'd have them kill the engines right there and just float
between two worlds   where i want to be and where i don't

want to be   looking at the banks of new london   so
close   so close   keeping this feeling rolling in my
chest

and it's also a lot like an inspection day   all hustle bustle
  fixing each other's duck caps   brushing the lint off each
other's uniform   everyone forgetting who they hate and
who they're pissed at   all working together to get through
this thing   that's how it feels now   everything's
exaggerated   bigger and brighter than most other days   so
clear it hurts my eyes   the ocean's bluer   the sky's bigger
  everyone around me is so familiar that i almost don't know
who they are

it's like watching speed being lowered into a well   first the
boat disappears   then his waist is gone   his chest   finally
his head   i look over the side to make sure the ocean hasn't
swallowed him   he stands in the small boat that hovers just
above the water   the keel inches from getting wet like a kiss
that's not quite there   speed signals to ericson   the lines
on deck are slacked and the boat settles into the ocean
making giant rings   i don't know if it's an illusion or i just
lose concentration but i can never see a ring die out i pick
one and follow its path but somehow it gets all mixed up the
farther it goes and then it's gone   speed kicks the engine
to life   blue smoke escapes from the water line   fumes rise
from the engine and sit lazily in the windless air surrounding
him in a filthy haze

the old man looks down from the bridge wing officers
huddle around like chicks to a hen   some trying to be
close   others keeping their distance   and chief wheeler
with his little green book paces the deck near us   making
notes   putting a word in here and there   pointing at
something and issuing some bullshit command   'check that

equatorial rhythms

line rat' 'watch the bow of the small boat ericson' 'keep
your hands inside the boat speed' like we're new at
this like we haven't done this a million times without him
saying a word but it's his moment to show he's in
charge grab some serious brownie points

ericson looks over the side

> you all set speed

speed gives him the thumbs up

> ok boys   time for victory at sea
> let's go rat   speed's waitin' on ya

i lower myself down the rope ladder   making sure of each
step   being more careful than usual   the small boat
rocks below me   i watch it swing from side to side   and
then i drop onto the deck   the first step is always
unsteady   like i've lost my sea legs   not used to the sharp
pitching of the small boat   i crawl forward and grab a
seat   the non-skid scrapes my ass through my pants   i look
over the side at the deep blue sea   i dip a hand into the
water

kelly drops into the boat   then rodgez   and holmes
he's lost his sense of humor again or maybe he never really
got it back   he looks up at the owasso a moment and turns
away and finds a seat aft   kelly and i sit at the bow   rodgez

sits in the middle   kelly turns and i can see a book sticking out of his back pocket   i have to smile   maybe he's planning on talking fine literature with some drug traffickers   or it's a good luck charm   or maybe it just protects his ass from the non-skid   two snipes drop into the boat   callini and someone else   a tall blonde guy   i never did get his name   he looks so pale and young   especially next to callini with his dark skin and beard so heavy his face looks blue   they take seats on either side of rodgez   and the rifles are lowered into the boat

cast off all lines

kelly tosses the painter off   holmes releases the line aft   i watch the ropes slap against the ship as they're hauled up the ladder inches its way along the hull   it disappears onto deck   strange being out here on the small boat everything so big   the sky   the ocean   from up on the owasso the rolling hide of the sea looks smooth and tame   but down here it's a mass of huge blue swells   i'm amazed we don't tip over   and the owasso towers overhead reflecting a painful white from the sun

 i close my eyes for a moment   get some relief from the burning rays   and when i open them again everything is blurred by tears

speed guns the engine and we leave the owasso   each turn of the screw moving us farther away from its familiar decks   i

equatorial rhythms

look back   a couple of the guys are waving   chief wheeler
watches from the lifeline with his hat tipped back   and
the old man stares at us through binoculars with his little
chicks huddling close by

speed stares straight ahead   in a trance   his face
serious   eyes hidden behind sunglasses   drops of sweat
lining his face   silently rodgez passes out the rifles that have
been neatly stacked on deck   kelly accepts his without a
word   lays it across his knees   barely touches it with one
hand

i grab the old m1   how serious it is now   it provided some
big-time laughs earlier   but now it feels heavier than
before   humorless   cold   deadly   what'll i do if things
go bad   how do i pull the trigger and blow someone's life
away   erase his future   maybe it'll be instinctive
 maybe the threat of harm will be all i need to pull the
trigger   not even give it a second thought

the snipes watch us handle the weapons

   hope you guys are ready for some action

it's the guy whose name i don't know   blondie   i guess he
means well   trying to make small talk   maybe a little
scared   but he gets no response   even callini turns and
faces away from him   the guy looks down and lets his smile
slowly drop onto the deck

we close in on the disabled vessel   it's a fishing boat   sixty
feet or so   maybe an old shrimp boat   i guess it used to
be white   it's mostly rust now   top to bottom   stem to
stern   as we get closer the hull looks like broken skin
diseased   reminding me of pictures in a high school
textbook of smallpox   large blisters bursting open   ripped
leaking skin engulfing the boat   a plague   with a smell
reaching out from the decomposing hull   exhaling a foul
breath that travels on a light breeze into my face   i can't tell
if it's some type of rotting food or rotting flesh or maybe even
escaping fuel fumes   or all three   i can see it though   it's a
yellow fog rising in waves to the sun   i wonder what
the ocean will do with this vessel   let it move about
shedding it's damaged skin   or is the sea gathering its
strength in some distant latitude   building a force that will
place its heavy feet on this vessels chest and push it to the
bottom   crush the life out of it   and then begin the slow
process of breaking it apart bit by bit   taking out what good is
left and feeding sea creatures below   disgorging the rest

we pull within a few yards of the boat

a face becomes visible on deck   suddenly   like a ghost   as
old and worn as the ship itself   a skeleton with dried black
leathery skin stretched over bone   patches of pink showing
through short curly hair   his face expressionless as a
statue   he stares at us with yellow eyes   and speaks with a
voice as lifeless as his face

come here wid da bow   over dis way

he holds a line in his hand   speed idles the boat down so
we're just gliding

      the line is tossed onto the bow   i hesitate an instant   if
i grab this line everything changes   the world will never be
same for me   maybe not for anyone   speed puts the
boat in reverse   stops inches from the bleeding hull   i
pick up the line and secure it to the cleat   the man on deck
moves slowly aft   another line sails through the air   floats
down to holmes   speed checks the boat fore and aft   the
sun shines off his skin like polished ebony   the dark glasses
an odd extension of his face   his powerful body anchored to
the bottom of the boat by his wide stance   i've never seen
him this serious before   it makes me antsy   like seeing a
parent scared for the first time

a rope ladder comes over the side and somehow i'm voted to
go first   not that anybody's said anything one way or the
other   but it's right next to me   and everyone else is
waiting   i take a deep breath   if i speak my voice will
shatter break apart like glass   my back is soaked with
sweat   fear or heat   bullshit   i know   i sling the
rifle over my back   a wave comes from nowhere and rocks
the boat forcing me to grab for the ladder   it catches my
hand i pull myself up and start climbing   straight toward
the sun   if trouble's on the way it'll be the moment i touch
deck   and i'll be helpless naked except for the rifle on my
back   that i'll never get to in time

a short thin man is waiting as i step onto the deck   his skin is
an odd color   gray   or maybe like a greenish gray   like a
rodent with its fur peeled off and then lightly baked over a
fire   i can't tell if he's black or white or hispanic or
whatever   his short black hair is cut uneven   as if someone
put a knife to it   his nose and face are long and thin with
tiny black eyes   and thin eyebrows   like a woman's
something that's been trimmed   he has no beard at all   or
maybe i just can't see it against his weird skin   he wears
baggy khaki pants and a white shirt open halfway down his
smooth chest   i sling the rifle off my shoulder and cradle it in
my arms

he extends a hand

        jean-francois toulet

        i'm first class petty officer callini

callini's climbed up close after me   he's rescued me from
having to answer the rodent   from having to touch his skin

the other snipe is next to callini   kelly comes up and stands
across from me putting the rodent and the snipes between
us   holmes touches the deck and moves directly to the
bow   rodgez stands next to the snipes

        i em very sorry to bodder you wid dis
        leetle problem   we could have managed
        i'm sure   but now dat you are here

he lets the words trail off

    `dis is my first mate`   `elty`

i'm not sure if it's LT like the letters or some type of
name   he's been standing back a ways and now steps
forward   he's big not tall short really but powerful big
mounds of muscles bulge from his arms   biceps straining
the red and white tee shirt like his insides are trying to bust
out of the skin   his hair is black and hangs halfway down his
forehead   almost touching the thick eyebrows or
eyebrow   it's one long line of black hairs   dark rings circle
the eyes set deep into his skull   his pants may have been
white once   a long time ago   before i was born   they're
filthy soiled with oil and dirt and who knows what else
  displaying their history   if you could study them closely
you'd know everything there is to know about this ape   if
anyone would really care   but i guess i do now   because
he's massive and he's here

    `where's the problem mr toulet`

callini's cool   keeping his voice calm and steady   he gives
the ape man a quick glance and then returns to the guy he
really has to deal with

    `dis way monsieur callini`

the rodent and callini and blondie and rodgez disappear
down a hatch   the sun falls heavily on me   i want to

wipe my face   but i don't want to seem frightened
  especially to elty   i don't want him to think i can't do my
job   i see kelly's not concerned about that   not feeling a
need to impress anyone   he runs a red bandanna across his
forehead and then wipes his glasses and replaces them
carefully on his nose

a couple other men are on deck   just sitting   one on the
bow   one to the left of me   i'm pretty sure he's the one
who tossed us the lines   an old face on a skinny little body
  i bet this guy doesn't touch a hundred   not much left
besides miserable eyes looking out from black weathered skin
with wrinkles so deep they're caverns running up and down
his face   he sits and looks at me   at kelly   at holmes   at the
sea   tattered clothes   more like rags held together by dirt
pants open at the crotch   no zipper   a black hole where it's
hard to tell if he even has underwear   his shirt has no
sleeves it's filthy pieces of cloth tied at the corners   just
enough to remain on his body   he has no hat so he shields
his eyes from the sun   squinting hard   looking through slits
and the weird pink patches on his scalp   like someone's
rubbed away the black   i look at the skin on this guy's legs
  near the ankles   they're rubbed pink like the patches on his
head   but different   like a band of some kind was wrapped
around the skin   worn for a long time   and just recently
released   with open sores that're leaking   pinkish   a
mixture of blood and something else   and scabs   he looks
down

wraps his hands around his knees like he's cold   and
there's the same bands of pink around his wrists   only
smaller   what's this guy been up to

jesus   irons

they keep these poor bastards in irons   i look at kelly to
see if he's noticed but he's just wiping his glasses again
  what the fuck   is this guy a prisoner   and who's the
rodent think he is   a fucking buccaneer   i have to
physically control my breathing   take one gulp of air at a
time   swallow the filthy smell   and i wish i could stop
sweating   but the sun's really doing a job on me   i want
to speak to this guy   ask him what's going on   what's
with the marks on his legs and arms   ape man sees me
eyeing the guy's legs and coughs real loud   getting my
attention   he lights a cigarette and drops the match at his
feet   i wait   but i don't think elty's gonna talk to me   too
much effort   used up all his words over his quota and now
has to rest his voice   he takes a deep drag   blowing up his
chest giving me a good look at the powerful muscles
straining to be released   he stares at me   i think for a second
the irons could have been his idea   but now it seems unlikely
  too much thought for this primate   it's got to be the rodent

i can hear it   hey elty i think we need to restrain the
crew   keep them from swimming a few hundred miles to
shore   put these irons on them   and the ape does it
  thinking it a good idea   thinking it'll keep these wretched
bodies from escaping to freedom   i want to say
something i don't know what   just something

but the sun blazes down on me   and i'm feeling better that
there won't be any violence   ape man is under orders to
keep an eye on us   show off his muscles   but that's it   and
the crew have left their fight somewhere in the distant past
  back in their youth   and i've no courage for asking what
these guys are up to   the less said the better   so the
silence continues   just the occasional slap of wave against
the peeling hull   i hide behind the quiet   it's
comfortable   making this whole thing go a lot easier

elty strolls to the bow   making sure the other member of the
crew isn't getting ready to jackknife into the atlantic and do a
quick breast stroke back home   flexing a little for
holmes   sucking on another cigarette

and then there's a whisper   it could be the light breeze that's
been carrying the smell of the ship to my nose   or maybe it's
speed on the two way radio down in the small boat   i take a
quick look over the side   he's just sitting there   and then
there's the noise again   carried by the wind over the port
side   i look down at the man closest to me   he's still about
eight or ten feet away   legs drawn up to his chest   staring out

to sea   his lips don't move at all   but the wind has shifted
slightly   and there's no doubt   it's him   i look up to check
on the ape and he's staring over holmes' shoulder toward the
owasso   and then there's this light voice drifting to my ears
  carrying a heavy load   breaking its back

    `help me`

twenty four

we've drifted around so that the owasso is now out of sight
   somewhere on the other side of the rusted hull   speed sets
the boat in motion   we move smoothly through the ocean
   and on the stern of the death boat are the remains of black
lettering   'sea devil'   barely visible   soon to be
overwhelmed by the approaching disease   the bursting skin
already distorting many of the letters   and from above the
dying hull appears the face of the man who asked for my
help   his eyes and face still blank   not expecting help from
the human race anymore   not expecting me to be any
different   the man's features become lost as we pull farther
away   but the scars on his ankles and wrists burn into my
head

everyone in the small boat is silent   even blondie is deep
in thought   i wonder what ghosts invade their heads

i try to peel the nightmare of the sea devil off   but it clings
to me   holds me tight   if i could remove its grip it would
peel away my skin   rip my muscles   reveal my bones
   my blood   my thoughts

equatorial rhythms

a line is tossed to me

the ladder lowered

we climb aboard the owasso

 and in the distance black smoke rises into the air as the sea
devil motors away   farther into its own nightmare   farther
into mine

equatorial rhythms

one

i'm lined up behind kelly   he looks odd without his
glasses   standing there in his underwear   squinting at the
fantail where a sailor steps forward and a slimy mixture is
dumped on him mostly garbage   leftovers from the
galley   it's in this guys hair   it's splattered all over his
body   dripping like a melting skin running onto the deck
  forming little puddles   the guy holds his arms and legs out
from his body   he's about to say something   just starting to
open his mouth and then a blast of salt water hits his body
shattering the muck into millions of tiny particles   he
almost falls   catches himself with a hand on the deck before
he goes down   he looks like a crab now crawling around on
all fours until he regains his balance   stands back up   and
another fist of water pounds him in the chest

we've crossed the equator

and it's hump day   initiation day   all the first timers get
dumped on

   and anyone who hasn't crossed the equator gets it today
too   that's why kelly and i are here   why we're standing in

line waiting for the garbage treatment   it's our first
crossing   it's almost everyone's first crossing so the stream
of sailors snakes up the starboard side   standing there in their
underwear waiting their turn   i wonder what this sight
looks like from above   what a gull looking down from high
over the ship would think   all these half-naked sailors
standing on deck   waiting to have garbage dumped on
them   and then be pulverized by a fire hose

two

kelly and i lather up in the shower   the bastards are
pumping in salt water so it's like scrubbing with a wire brush

         i wondah how hump days goin'   could be
         interestin' with all these cadets heah

         i understand they've removed them from the
         lower elements

         hiding 'em with the officahs huh

         they're having their own hump day

kelly points his face at the spraying water   still looking odd
without his glasses   it's strange how we're going through
this again   the first time was just out of boot camp   boots
   hump day a real shock   neither one of us knowing what to
expect   not even knowing each other   and then in this same
shower   getting cleaned up just like now   talking a little
   and finally laughing   kelly starting it   just laughing   and
infecting me   until the two of us can barely stand   not

knowing if it was water or tears on his face at one point
    he's amazing   so intelligent so well read and yet he's
just one of the guys he fits in everywhere everyone likes
him officers snipes all the deckies everyone takes to him
  something i never feel

everything's always so odd for me around people like i'm an
outsider   someone that floats in and out of their
world   but i have my moments like sitting in some quiet
corner with kelly and talking sports or music or ships or
whatever i'll feel that i'm alive a real person with the rest
of the world a giant black orb circling somewhere off in the
distance in those moments i feel almost happy with my life
in the service with my life aboard ship my life at sea my
life   but sooner or later someone barges into this world
and reality swoops down and swallows me gulps me into its
belly   so i pull myself away make myself disappear take a
few steps back or go lay in my rack or melt into a
bulkhead   it's not like i want to be this way but it's how
i feel it's the way i do things   it's the way i get through a
life once so foreign that i thought death would be better than
facing another day

      i heard the offisahs planned that little
      gahbage and hose operation

      that's what i heard too   it was okay i
      guess   could've been a lot worse

      like what's probably goin' on right now

we dry off   kelly puts his glasses on and once again becomes
kelly   his lips wired into a boyish grin   towel wrapped
around his waist   he grabs his shaving kit and waves an arm
at me

come on slick

three

kelly and i walk down the ladder to the snipes quarters   it's
a nightmare   a vision of hell   or a twisted minds idea of
fun   it's hump day   different types of music scream
through the air crashing against each other   engaged in
hand-to-hand combat   smoke circles the area reflecting
blue light drawing twisted shapes   ghostly patterns dancing
to the wild music   in the middle of the deck a sailor's held
down   two guys are kneeling on his arms and two are
sitting on his legs his face is red   he's breathless a huge
vein pops out of his neck like a bulging tunnel white against
the red skin   he's scared   pissed off and wants to escape
the madness   but a short squatty snipe stands over him
   blonde beard thick and wild a primitive mask   he grabs
the guys belt and yanks up on it   he inserts a grease gun and
opens fire

in a corner is a group of five or six   they've surrounded
tuttleman   he's hated by the snipes   acts like he knows
everything   acts like a big shot   but worst of all he's gone to
officers thinking it was in private   that their meetings
would be kept secret   passing the word about alcohol and

drugs among the crew   trading in a few snipes for some
favors that don't really add up to much but must make
tuttleman feel important   tears dance off his white face
 his lips are red like he's wearing lipstick   the crowd turns
him around exposing his back   it looks like it was used for a
pin cushion   red welts dotted everywhere some turning blue
some with tiny dots of blood sitting on them   a hand raises
to shoulder height   a belt drips from it   there's a
pause   i watch the thick smoke circle around a head
 i hear a screeching laugh from the other side of the quarters
   and the belt whips down onto bare flesh with a brutal snap
of skin followed by a scream   and a useless plead for mercy

kelly and i move down another level   the pit's not much
better in fact it looks even worse   the smoke is thicker a
brownish yellow   the heat's stripped the crew to the
waist   naked torsos shining polished with sweat   and
the music's overpowering rock and roll thunder smashing its
head against the bulkhead ripping through my ears   i
can see bottles being passed between the racks going from
one hand to the next   going from one set of lips to the next
   head thrown back   the booze bubbling in the bottle as it
goes down a throat and then passed on   a new guy lies
on the deck   it's stevens   he's on watch duty this trip so i
haven't seen him much   in fact i'd forgotten all about him
   he lies on the deck naked except for the underwear stuck to
his skin   a dirty bandanna's tied across his eyes   leblanc sits
on his arms and chest   he spoons some soggy stuff out of a
bowl and places it on stevens lips   the guy gags   it's not so

much from what it is   it's what it might be that's so terrifying
i know how he feels   the black tunnel   the strange sounds
    the weight on your chest visions of insects or garbage
touching your tongue   it's the worst of fears   the unknown

```
    eat it stevens!       eat it!
```

stevens opens his mouth just a sliver   the spoon is forced in
and the food dropped down   a look of disgust covers his face
as he chews the stuff   and then swallows

rodgez looks down at leblanc

```
    thethethe that's enough leblanc
    steven's a preeeeetty good guy    for a
    boot
```

leblanc smiles and nods at rodgez and takes the blindfold off
the stricken face   he gets off his chest and reaches a hand to
stevens and helps him stand   leblanc rubs his stubby
fingers in the boot's hair

```
    congratulations kid       you're part a the
    crew

    youyouyouyouuuuuuuummmmmmmade it kid    hehe
```

stevens looks around like he doesn't believe it's over   waiting
for something else to happen waiting for someone else to pin

him to the deck and make him eat something disgusting
   but there is no more   so a smile makes its way onto his face

```
what was that shit you fed me

don't ask kid    don't ask    go take a
shower and i'll get you a coke to wash it
down

hey   thanks leblanc
```

stevens goes to his locker he grabs a bar of soap and a towel
and heads for the showers   smiling all the way like he was
just on a picnic   it's strange   the whole thing's horrible at
the time   but when you finally make it through there's a
sense of pride that goes with having survived it   and a
feeling of camaraderie   of brotherhood   they've taken this
abuse before you and now you've taken it too   and now
you're one of them   it's an awkward definition of
belonging   but it's true   and it makes you happy   at
least for the moment

leblanc puts his hands on me and kelly

```
lets go see how ericson's doin'
```

in the opposite corner a block and tackle's been fastened to
the overhead   hanging from it's a naked body   like
meat drooping from a hook   white except for the tanned

arms and neck   hands tied   the body turns slowly as if
being basted over an open fire   until the tear stained face of
holmes passes before me   and then spins away   ericson
watches the body his eyes circled in red dreamy with booze
touched with madness   he's mesmerized by the figure that
spins in front of him   can't take his eyes off it   without
looking away he grabs a bottle of tabasco sauce off the deck
and opens it   then he pours it onto holmes' balls   shaking
the bottle   i wince at the sight   i feel the pain   but i
don't make a move to stop him i don't open my mouth and
tell him that's enough i just stand there while the music
screams from the bulkhead and the sickly yellow fog dances
around the pit and the booze drains down throats   i feel
like grabbing the tabasco sauce and pouring it down ericson's
throat   watch him turn red   watch him grab his face and
run for the head   watch him get deathly sick

instead i just watch

ericson squats and looks at the dirty face hanging upside
down

        fuckin boot!

as holmes continues to spin   and not a sound comes from
his mouth   like and old weathery face from a rusted hull
that's given up hope

four

the day room's packed   levine and sampson play guitars
  sending out sweet notes   so clear and distinct i feel i could
snatch each one out of the air and hold it   kelly looks up a
moment at the two musicians   a grin on his face like a little
boy   he turns and nods at me   buries his gaze once more in
the book held against his knees   the rest of the crew watch
the musicians   most of them anyway   some look at their
hands   others have their eyes closed   sleeping or just
thinking   letting the music invade their heads   i spot a
couple of new guys   you can't miss the glow on their faces
  the brightness in their eyes   not sitting here as strangers
anymore   now citizens of the owasso   members of this
vagabond family in the middle of the atlantic   sitting on top
of the equator

the music stops   weak applause   smoke escapes from
mouths and drifts up into the thick cloud that hangs
overhead

levine and sampson start another song

i tap kelly on the shoulder and stand   he nods   i leave

out on deck the tropical warmth is soft as a naked woman   a
silky body   brushing her red lips across my face   her
breasts against my chest   her legs between my legs   with
thousands of tiny eyes   high up in the sky   sprinkled
everywhere

two sailors walk past in the dark   without a word   and
then disappear

the moon drops silver onto the ocean   letting it roll and
dance on the waves

```
                    five
```

drifting

it's a strange feeling   bobbing on the rising shoulders of the
sea   each swell raising the owasso up   and then easing her
back down   i miss the forward movement   the power of
the engines   the deep rumble of the diesels from below
  like a kitten purring when you hold on to its body
    the sound of life

six

chief wheeler walks over to me   his shirt stuck to his
back   deep brown with sweat little green book in
hand   wearing a look that i can't read

    rat   go down to the engine room and
    find out what's going on

    you mean we're not supposed to be
    stopped   this isn't part of hump day
    giving the snipes some time off

he looks up at the heartless sun   squinting his eyes   his
head more out to sea than with me

    no   we should be under way

and he continues to look at the sky   maybe for signs of
clouds   or a passing shower to wash the sweat from the
owasso

the heat flexes its muscles   presses its powerful hands over
my mouth and against the sides of my head
squeezing   squeezing

and the heat gets worse as i drop farther into the bottom of
the ship   each step down like lowering myself into a grave
 a grave placed in the center of a furnace   flames licking the
steel

pipes and fittings and gears and levers crisscross everywhere
  above me below me   all around me   mostly silver
sometimes red   like a huge erector set   i walk onto a
metal platform   a path through the silent machinery   a
roadway through the ship's intestines   with the heat pulling
the sweat from my body   creating hundreds of tiny rivers
that flow down my face and back and under my arms and
down my legs   i walk carefully along making sure i don't
touch anything   don't lean on anything   in case it's hot or
fragile or a switch to a box that does something nobody
wants done right now   this whole place overwhelms me
  scares me   makes me feel like i'm locked in a giant closet or

buried underground   waiting for the air to run out
these guys work down here   sometimes eat down here   live
down here   i wonder why they do it what makes them so
different from me

i walk around a corner   a body lies across the walkway   head
and chest under a huge diesel   legs lying across my path the
filthy pants looking as if they've been dipped in lighter fluid
that kind of dangerous wet look

a hand holds onto a pipe gripping it so tight the skin is white

i kneel down

    `mcgregor`

nothing

    `mcgregor`

the body works itself painfully out   the huge stomach
bouncing ripples of fat walking from the center out to the
sides and then disappearing   his chest is a forest of red
hairs   matted with grease and sweat and dirt plastered to
the skin creating a kind of scarlet paisley pattern   and then
mcgregor's head comes into view   his beard sticking out at
me   thousands of tiny crimson snakes interlaced in some
demented dance   slick with sweat and grease   with the skin
around his eyes and forehead almost black like he's wearing
a mask

94

```
what the fuck man

chief wheeler wants to know if there's a
problem     he doesn't think this shutdown
was scheduled

what the fuck rat     what's it look like
asshole     hey fuck you!     and fuck
chief wheeler!
```

he starts to slide under the engine   face red with anger
he hesitates a moment   and then pulls himself out and
stands up   like an old man   like every muscle in his body
hurts   letting out a deep sigh   running a huge forearm
across his face

```
hey rat     you're okay     i don't mean
nothin' 'bout you
```

he wipes his hands on a filthy rag

```
the fucking diesels er down     both of
'em     we brought 'em down for hump day
and now we can't bring'em back up     the
old man's all over our ass     i thought
he was gonna have a stroke right there
when chief and callini and i were in his
cabin     that dude is one scary fucker
rat     i mean it
```

```
how long we gonna be down

shit    wish i knew    tell you the truth
rat    i can't even find the problem yet
it's like the fucking ship decided it's
had enough and just isn't goin' any
farther
```

the sweat rolls down his temple   gathering black dirt and
grease along the way

  he looks down at the deck   rubs a spot with his foot   runs
a hand through the red snakes on his face   and then his eyes
roll my way   looking tired   looking lost

```
hey rat     keep this to yourself man okay
even the chief doesn't know i can't find
the problem    told him i was pretty sure
i knew what it was
```

he keeps wiping his hands

```
really thought i did    shit rat     i
don't know now    i just don't know
```

he looks down at the rag that continues to roll his hands
  then he looks at me

```
fuck it's hot down here    i sent
crossman and thin man up for some air and
```

```
a drink     maybe they'll come up with
somethin' while they're takin' a break
```

he doesn't look like he believes it though   two years on the
owasso   he knows these engines better than he knows his
wife's body   the tiny woman who comes to greet him when
we pull into port and wave goodbye when we set sail   i
always wonder how they got together   how she supports this
huge mass of flesh during sex   the little girl with the bossy
mouth   pointy little tits that seem to accuse me of something
when they're aimed my way   she seems to purposely put
mcgregor down in front of everyone   little jabs   did you fix
anything today or is it still broken   take a shower before you
come up to see me   tiny words like darts   right between the
eyes   i'll bet he knows his engines better than he knows her

```
fuck it's hot rat
```

mcgregor lowers himself down   and returns to his sick
diesels

eight

the sun follows me around the deck   its blinding light
bounces off the white superstructure piercing my eyes
  making them water   my shirt clings to my body with
thousands of wet fingers   rubbing   chafing   pulling at my
skin   waves of heat rise from the deck making everything
blurred

the crew moves slower as the day goes on   finally stopping
when the sun roars down from directly overhead   feeding
on the energy it sucks from us   growing stronger as we grow
weaker

everything's been turned off the lights the fans   even the
radar's off   and chief wheeler's nowhere to be found
maybe hiding in some corner of the ship   maybe finding a
piece of shade he doesn't want to share   reading his little
green book   making notes

the rest of us gradually move to the dark side of the ship
finding refuge from the relentless sun   but still having to deal
with the thick humid air   i look down the line of sailors

equatorial rhythms

sitting with their backs to the bulkhead   each body gasping
for breath   sweat falling onto the deck like drops of rain

my line of sight rises to the bridge wing   where the old man
stares down at us

nine

sleep's impossible   the pit's a sauna   everything's soaked
clothes   sheets pillows mattresses   even the deck has a
thin coat of something like oil on it from ages of ground in
dirt   mixing with the humidity and floating to the surface   i
had to skate more than walk across it   and it's so quiet
now   like a hospital but without the moaning of the sick
without any talking at all it's dead   and black except for
gomez' weak light   maybe everyone's waiting for something
to happen   waiting for the rumble of the engines
thinking it must be just around the corner   any minute now
and we'll be under way driving through the sea

gomez sits on the deck by his rack   an emergency lantern
struggles against the dark   lighting his face and hands
putting blurry shadows against the bulkhead   his delicate
fingers wrap thin pieces of string over and under and around
each other   creating a kind of net   it could be a piece of art
could be on display at some museum   he pauses   looks at
his work closely   squinting into the anemic light   a drop of
water falls from his nose   he grabs another piece of string
and his fingers dance some intricate pattern i can't follow

equatorial rhythms

moving too fast for me   then he stops wipes his forehead
holds his work in his hand   stares at it without expression for
a second   and tosses it down in disgust

```
    fuckin shit!       i'm never makeen thees
    many meestakes before            never!
```

he jumps to his feet   climbs the ladder   a wake of spanish
flows out behind him the words fat and heavy   pounding
onto the slippery deck

```
    puta!
```

and a voice comes from the opposite end of the pit

```
    fuckin' aye gomez
```

ten

i make my way out of the pit   vomited out by the humidity
and the foul stench it's breeding

everything's so silent   as if the heat has pushed all noise
back into the human beings and holds its heavy hand against
everyone's mouth   preventing any speech   any noise

the deck is littered with bodies sailors lying around like
scattered blue logs   trying to catch a breeze or at least avoid
the decaying of the quarters below

the sun's gone   swallowed by the sea and the black sky   but
the night remains heated   and the wind is nowhere to be
found   i feel abandoned   left to this sweltering spot at
the center of the earth   hot air rising from its navel
surrounded by a dark voluptuous skin with the cooling
breezes passing far overhead   blurring the moon and stars

there's a shifting of bodies   a restless attempt at sleep

the moon shows on kelly's face   his glasses tipped down on

his nose   he nods and says 'rat' and sits next to me with his
back to the lifelines   and shifts his book around to catch the
full light of the moon

little things   it strikes me that little things like no light for
reading   may drive us all mad

muster   lined up like toys   the morning sun already
powerful on the back of my neck

chief wheeler paces nervously   constantly wiping sweat
from his face with a soaked handkerchief   he shades his
eyes looks toward the bow   and then turns back to us

all hands attention on deck

we stand straight as flagpoles   inflexible   unmoving
squeezing the life out of ourselves for one man   the
captain walks our way   his long lean body hunched over
  as if he has to carry the ship and its crew on his back as if
he has the earth balanced on his shoulders   he salutes the
chief and then walks along the human wall   each sailor
getting a stare as the old man searches for imperfections
looking for unshined shoes or dangling threads or a dull belt
buckle   he lingers over each sailor   takes in every detail
about him   makes him as uncomfortable as possible   and
then moves to the next victim   one after the other   until he
stops in front of me   and stares with deep sunken eyes set so

far back the sockets are black   he stoops so that his huge
head is directly in front of me   his face long and narrow the
skin hanging limply from his jaw wrinkled   leathery   like
the sun has started to mummify him   not waiting for death
not waiting for him to be buried   his dried lips form a
square deep lines of puckered skin frame his mouth   huge
yellow teeth stand jaggedly next to each other   the earth
stops rotating   and then he moves on

the sun continues to rise   and i'm wilting   sinking into the
deck under the heat waiting for my legs to give way
wondering how much it'll hurt when i hit the deck
wondering if they'll just leave me there until inspection's over

but the old man finishes and i'm still on my feet   he moves to
the center of the deck and stands before us   looking serious
like what we do here matters a shit to the rest of the world
like passing inspection will bring about world peace or
having shined shoes will end hunger   and of course the
chief stands next to him fingering his little green book
pouring sweat onto the deck like he's sprung a leak   and
always ready to kiss the old man's ass

the captain's mouth opens and the yellow teeth let the deep
rumbling voice escape

        i'm giving all of you the same message i
        gave the rest of the crew

```
        you are sailors in the united
states coast guard     you will behave as
such      you are to remain in uniform at
all times     shirt     pants     boots
caps
```

his long bony hands lace into each other the skin so wrinkled
it looks dirty

```
this is not a cruise ship      we are not
here to get a tan     we are here to work
to teach the cadets how to be better
sailors
```

i notice for the first time how clean his uniform is   the folds
razor sharp   his officer's cap sitting squarely on his bony
head   and i notice he's not sweating i can't even see a bead
on his forehead

```
i will confirm the rumors right now      we
will not radio for help     radio
communications have been halted to save
power     we will get this ship up and
running    and we will continue on our own
without outside help     i have never
called for help my entire career    and i
will not start now because of the
incompetence of this crew     i
will      not      get that straight in
```

```
your heads right now     you will do your
job    and keep this vessel shipshape
just as engineering will do their job
and get this ship under way
```

he pauses a moment   a single drop of sweat clings to his
temple

```
i will not have a breakdown in this ships'
discipline
```

he salutes chief wheeler then turns and walks back toward
the bridge melting into the waves of heat   and i feel like
i'm watching death go back to its hole

twelve

another sweltering day   even worse than yesterday if that's
possible   two cadets are painting on the fantail one is
harvey   still working hard at being one of the guys   trying
to fit in   he sways a little   like someone's moving the earth
under him   then he rocks back and sits on the deck   a look
of surprise on his face   with the paint brush still in his
hand   and then he falls over   not a word of
complaint not even a moan   he just stops functioning   like
he's run out of gas   i race over and kneel next to his body
it's drenched in sweat   boiling hot to the touch   i start to
tell the other guy to go get help   but he's stretched out on the
deck himself grabbing for breath   like a fish out of the
ocean

chief wheeler's at the starboard small boat

        chief!   chief!   these guys have
        passed out

he hurries over and looks at me   at harvey   at the other guy
he stands there for a second looking puzzled   then he

takes a few steps to port and looks up at the bridge wing and
comes back and stands directly over harvey

```
get up!     get up quickly!     now
sailor      get up!    he may see you
get up get up get up
```

he takes another look at the bridge wing and comes back

```
let's go men    up up up

chief!    they're passed out    they need
help
```

gomez comes around the corner

```
whas goeen on

they're passed out gomez     go get the
doc man    quick
```

he runs to a hatch and then disappears inside   chief
wheeler continues to stare at the fallen sailors   looking scared
he opens his little green book and starts making notes
maybe jotting down what happened   maybe noting that he
tried to get these guys up covering his ass   while harvey and
the other cadet roast in the sun

the mess hall's a steam bath   soaked shirts stick to bodies
sweat traces lines through dirty faces   everyone looks twenty
years older

mcgregor sits alone   making notes on a sweat soaked piece
of paper like trying to write under water

some gunners mates are crowded at a table   picking at their
food   talking a little

a group of radarmen sit across from mcgregor   complaining
about the heat   about how hot it is in the radar room
wondering why they have to take shifts in there when
everything's turned off anyway   but they're always bitching
about something   even in the best of times   one guy folds
a napkin into a tiny square   another plays with the bill of his
cap creasing the edges over like he's on a baseball team
then one of them looks at mcgregor   a little guy   i don't
know his name but i recognize him because he's always
talking about the women he's slept with   a blonde here   a
redhead there   this one was great   that one was a virgin

that's all he has to say   so now he looks at mcgregor a
second and then turns back to the other guys at the table

```
yeah    well     i wonder what's taking so
long to get the fucking engines running
if the radar was down this long the old
man would have court martialed us by now
```

the table goes silent

the gunners mates look up

the mess is a tomb

the little guy laughs or tries to   like he doesn't give a shit who
hears and then his lips slowly melt into a frown

mcgregor's skin turns red   his lips together   he turns the
pen in his hand until he's holding it like a knife   but his
eyes stay fixed on the paper

the asshole's right there   within reach   looking more than
just a little scared now   looking like he wants to put a hand
in the air and pull the words back into his mouth and
swallow them   and some weird sense of pride stops him
from rising from his seat and leaving so he sits and stares at
his hands not really knowing how to act   not knowing
what to say

i watch   and i hope   i hope mcgregor punishes this guy   i
hope he lets out his rage his frustrations   his longing for a
cool breeze and a full nights sleep   i want it for me as well as
him   i want him to beat the shit out of this guy because i'm
hot and tired and i don't like the little fucker and i just want
to scream at the sun for making me miserable

mcgregor snaps the pen in half   breaks its back   the ink
runs over his hand like blue blood   he looks out a porthole
maybe searching for an answer   maybe searching for a
wind to blow him away   maybe deciding how badly he'll
beat this little shit   holding some measuring stick up to
him   a day out of work   two   a week   maybe
longer   and all the time i'm pulling for violence   for
unrestrained anger   for release from any duty or honor   or
fear of punishment   for some kind of sick justice

mcgregor slowly rises   his massive chest plastered with swirls
of greasy red hairs   his mouth open slightly

he drops the crushed pen on the table and stares straight into
the eyes of the guy who'll soon crumble under his leaden fists
wishing he'd never seen mcgregor   never seen this crew
never set foot on this ship

and then mcgregor turns   and leaves

fourteen

the sun sits on the ocean   a giant red eye   seeping into the
water like an open wound   dyeing it crimson   it stares
at me   dares me to speak to it   howl at it   stop it from
falling into the ocean

everyone's on deck   shirts off   pant legs rolled up
looking for the wind   searching for a breeze that's strayed
across the wall of the equator   something to fill the
emptiness   the silence

the owasso rocks to port   reminding me i'm a sailor and not
just the survivor in a prison of heat

drops of sweat roll down my temple   stream down my
cheeks   and then fall onto my chest   slide down to my
stomach

i'm tired   drained   i don't want to get up anymore   i
don't think my legs have enough strength to lift me off the
deck   i just want to sleep   just sleep

footsteps   steady   rhythmic   strong

i turn my head toward the sound   and the old man comes
into view   shirt and pants neatly pressed   hat tipped a bit
to one side   kind of jaunty   out of character   he comes
closer   black eyes   leathery skin   jowls reaching for the
deck   lips turned slightly down   he stops in front of me
he moves his eyes over my head out to the endless rolling
ocean   and the crimson eye that sinks into the sea under his
dark gaze   i stare at his spit-shined shoes and how they
reflect the dying color of the sky   i've always been afraid of
people like him   people in power   people in charge   people
who act like they're better than everyone else   better than
me   maybe they are   right now i don't give a shit
i'm beyond caring   way beyond that   so maybe he'll say
something to me   try to make me put on my shirt   or try to
make me go sleep in the pit   or just try to make me do
something anything   and i'll find the strength to rise up and
beat him to a bloody paste   i can feel my fist crushing into
the dried skull   that look remaining on his face as knuckles
rain down   his teeth ripping the skin from my hands   the
yellow fangs stained with blood   the dead skin flapping
with each blow

equatorial rhythms

my heart races

my veins pulse

and then the shoes shift   and move away

fifteen

the night's a deep deep black   endless   a giant tunnel
swallowing the earth   and the stars are tiny guiding lights
that when we finally decipher the code will lead us home
they're so bright   pure white   and the moon drops
shadows across the deck   odd strips of black   dark soldiers
administering death by heat   the ocean moves slowly
an occasional swell like the bottomless breath of someone
deeply asleep   it's like standing on a giant heart   feeling
the steady rhythm of the earth   of the equator   it feels so
calm   so soothing   a gentle vibration   massaging
fingers   but it's a lie   a cheat   a trap   because
it's not just a single sound   it's many voices
hundreds   maybe thousands   distant screams
faraway howls of pain   begging for relief from the endless
black nights and white days   the voices filtered through a
wall of heat   merging into a choir   one sound   one
whispering wail of protest   a hypnotic tone that never
stops for breath   never sleeps   never ceases   never retreats

          it sucks the life from me with red sensuous lips
beautiful to look at but clammy and putrid to the touch

equatorial rhythms

and through those lips come the false rhythm   the
thousands of tortured screams   the unending voice of
hopelessness   the rhythm of death

the rhythm of the equator

sixteen

black   like the inside of an endless shaft
hopelessly long   that starts to spiral downward   and
jennifer's form comes into view   fading in   and out
  flowing   as though made of liquid   her figure constantly
changing   widening on one end   shrinking at another
  she pulls her hair back   her shoulders are tanned and
smooth   the color of wet sand   her skin is oiled shining
  highlighting the firm breasts   narrow hips   long legs
    her eyes look directly into me   heavy with makeup
  so close to me now   reflecting light from somewhere far in
the distance   her face pulls away   eyes half shut as
though she's having sex and loving it   feeling something
sensual on her body   and her arms rise in the air   hands
reaching over her head   framing her face   the tongue still
working around the hungry mouth   sweat running down
her naked body   tiny streams tracing lines on her face
moving over her breasts clinging to her nipples for a moment
and then plunging into the endless dark   the sweat
flowing freely over her body now over her thighs
disappearing in the thick mat of hair between her legs   and a
moan comes from her red lips a deep sensual sound and i

118

struggle to tell her i miss her i try to push the words out to her
but my voice is lost deep in my chest and her body gyrates
before me hips swirling and thrusting arms flowing sweating
becoming smaller and smaller and my chest about to collapse
from the pain of trying to call to her until a strange guttural
sound comes out   low and hoarse   and all i can say is
jennifer

            jennifer

                                jennifer

seventeen

i wake up   and wonder how long i've slept   thirty minutes
an hour   maybe two i don't know   but it's not long
enough to have gained any strength   any courage to fight
the equatorial heat   but maybe it's long enough to get
rid of the visions that stalk my head   haunt my brain
pounce on me when i least expect it   making me look
around embarrassed   as though someone can read my mind
or watch the ghosts dance across my face   but
they're gone   or maybe i just don't care anymore   i feel a
kind of strange peace   like there's a cease-fire in my head   a
truce   the memories don't seem as torturous now
don't feel like they'll crush my brain or break my spirit   i
feel different

 jennifer's gone   she didn't throw my faults in my face   but
she can't live with them   she needs something else
someone else

and my mother

my mother and her bottle and her boyfriends will never
change   she deals with the world in her own way   grabbing
for each moment of happiness   trying to remove the face of
one man   just for a second   so she can have a laugh or two

and my father   my father will never return to the living
his body's gone   his smile removed   i still see him   i still talk
to him   i still dream about him   but that's it   i can't shake
his hand or pat his back   hear his laugh   say good-bye

eighteen

i walk toward the bow   avoiding the protruding legs
attached to bodies that beg for sleep   i see three or four
shadows   they lean forward against the lifelines and piss
into the ocean below   i wonder if it's a bet they have   no
balls to piss over the side of the ship   see if an officer catches
them   or see whose stream can travel farthest   they stop
one by one   but there's no salty banter   no talk of who won
the bet   they just silently go back to their spot on deck
  looking for comfort   looking for sleep

i pass through a couple of hatches into the head
  emergency lanterns create little pockets of light   casting
shadows   black and gray   like a grainy photo   and
the stench is overpowering   unrelenting   urine and shit
mixed with heat and humidity   a sour smell   making
my eyes water   and my breath get stuck deep inside my
throat   i walk past the showers   a weak light falls across
naked bodies   just pieces of flesh   shiny with sweat standing
under dry shower heads   maybe a hand on a hip   or a
face pointed overhead   arms moving up and down   up
and down   each to a rhythm of its own   i turn to go to a

stall   but they're all taken   boondockers sticking out from
underneath   like some kind of comedy   a movie with all
the characters doing their thing and i'm the straight man   the
joke's on me   as the heat wrings sweat from my body and
drips down my arm pits   my hands   my face   trapped in a
stew of heat and humidity and an earth gone crazy with fever
stirred once in a while to keep the sickly brew fresh
   overwhelming the crew with desperation   the loneliness
and sleeplessness unbearable   and everywhere's the
sound of flesh on flesh   muted   whispered   is it
love   or self abuse   is it giving in   or surviving
   a slight moan comes from the shower   low   mumbled
      a noisy breath   as a sailor spills himself onto the owasso

nineteen

daylight   the sun's rising   it knows we're down   it
knows some of us are out   so it doubles its efforts
reaches deep down and gathers all its force   rolls itself into a
ball of white death and hurls pieces of itself at us   we're in an
oven

i wonder how mcgregor's doing   as he bakes under his
engines   swimming in grease and dirt   struggling to heal
the owasso   find the wound and clean it and get us back
under way

up on deck everyone's back on the shady side of the ship
some of the guys still pretend to work   sitting cans of paint
next to them   looking around occasionally   as if they're
fooling anyone   as if anyone cares any more

and chief wheeler passes by once in a while   mumbling to
himself   like he's memorizing something   a poem   a
prayer

and there's a voice from the forecastle   sounding desperate

```
chief!     chief!    quick!        down the
forward boatswains hole
```

```
what          what is it
```

```
chief quick!        it's holmes
```

i get to my feet and walk forward   wondering what's going
on   why all the commotion   guys are sliding down the
ladder   anxious to see for themselves   anxious to do
something besides wait for the ship to move   i climb down
the ladder   i walk through a hatch and there's a crowd
ahead   eight or nine guys creating a wall   watching   in
silence   except for the heavy breathing of someone
someone hidden by the wall   gasping for air

```
fuck you chief!
```

we all turn and look at the chief who's just come up to my
shoulder

and holmes' voice screams again

```
yeah that's right      fuck you chief!
i had no choice      i had no fucking
choice! and you know it!           fuck
you chief!
```

i turn to the voice i see holmes between the other heads

his eyes wide   his face a horrible mask of agony   his
hands are raised in the air   one holding a knife   blood
dripping from the blade   and at his feet lies a body   the
face turned away from me at an odd angle   staining the
coiled lines red

i feel the chief's hand touch my back   using me for
support   losing his sea legs   losing his life legs   and i
want to turn around and shout in his fucking face   see see i
told you   i told you i told you   but his voice is so weak
so drained   so pathetic that i can't bring myself to crush him
any more

```
i     i      i need to check this out
you'll have to come with me holmes
yes     yes       you'll need to follow me
and we'll have to look into this

look into what chief!    he followed me
followed me down here       wouldn't
leave me alone       wouldn't fucking leave
me alone for one minute      one minute!
fuck!
```

i turn and step back   removing the chief's hand from me
casting him adrift   as he opens his little green book   maybe
looking for some notes on what to do when someone's lost it
when one of your crew has left this world for another
when a sailor's mind has flown out over the ocean leaving his
body to do what it wants

and there's the sound of metal entering flesh   ripping
skin   severing veins

shouting no no no   the crew surges forward

sounds of surprise   curses

and through the legs of the wall before me i see the top of a
head and the blood dripping out onto the body below it

twenty

the sun rains down on my face   squeezing sweat from under
my duck cap   pushing sheets of water down my face that
fall somewhere onto the deck below   i look across at kelly
he looks as miserable as me   maybe worse   his glasses
have rivers running down the lenses   it must be like looking
under water   everything distorted   next to kelly is speed
next to me is rodgez   we balance a metal table that supports
a body with an american flag draped over it   it's weird
him being dead   i know he loved horses   he talked about
feeding them   the feel of their powerful bodies as he raced
from one end of the farm to the other   the smell of the barn
the hay   the horses   he had never even seen the ocean 'til he
joined the coast guard   i wonder what made him join
why he didn't go to college   or work on a farm   i guess he
didn't want to   maybe tired of school i know how that is
guess he wasn't too keen on going to vietnam   i can relate to
that too   so here he is   his body anyway   tissue rotting
under the intense heat   like it's being called back to
somewhere   to the sea

equatorial rhythms

gomez and leblanc and stevens and the chief are behind me
holding a metal table of their own   with the chaplain
standing over them   his words swimming through the
humidity   his voice deep and serious   with a touch of
emotion   like it's about to crack   but doesn't

then everything's still   silent

until there's movement behind me   and the sound of
disturbed water

ericson

the preacher moves over to us   stands in front of the body
with a bible in his hands   so i stare out over kelly's head
kind of entering into a trance   hypnotising myself so that
everything that's happening doesn't really sink in   the
preacher's words not penetrating my brain   just touching
my skull for an instant   maybe long enough for me to
recognize a word or two   and then moving on to someone
else   someone who'll pay attention   for me it's just words
'forgive' 'soul' 'this world' 'the next'   i wonder if
somewhere up in the sky this soul can understand all this
maybe he's smiling   maybe it's not so bad wherever he is
maybe he's at peace   even talking with ericson
communicating with him somehow   each saying they're
sorry   relieved they don't have to deal with each other on
earth any more   'our world'   'peace'   'forever'

the sun bakes my head   my shoulders   it cooks the flesh
before me   sending a putrid odor into the stale air

kelly takes a deep breath

rodgez wipes the sweat from his forehead

and then it's time   we lift the metal table and slide the body
over the side   through the heavy air   and into the mouth of
the waiting sea   listening to the splash of the ocean as it
falls through watery fingers to the cold black world below

holmes

it's like a sacrifice by an ancient tribe   human offerings
payment for sins   and something is accepting these
bodies   maybe the air licked the carcasses before they
entered the mouth of the ocean   and is satisfied that the
gifts are real   so it opens its heavy curtains and lets a soft
breeze blow onto my face   the gentle movement touching
my skin   my eyes   my mouth

the entire crew is now trying to drink the lightly moving
air   pushing their faces at the sky   nets of flesh trying to
catch wind

there's a rumbling under my feet it shakes my body for a
moment   and then stops   i look at the deck as if i've never
seen it before   as if it just swept down from another planet
and slid under my feet   it rumbles again   louder
longer   real   as the engines cough and hack   and
then grind to life

figurehead

one

the engines rumble under my feet   a powerful chest
bellowing with life   infecting me   infecting the
crew   even infecting the creatures below   i can taste their
life in the air   thick and salty

i stand by the lifelines and watch the owasso cut through the
ocean   feel the power as we slash our way to rio

rodgez and kelly walk along the deck side by side   kelly
tips his cap to me   his glasses clean and shiny a book in his
hand a bandanna sticking out from his back pocket   the
bookworm among the illiterate   saneness in the middle of
insanity   rodgez smiles at me   pressing the freckles on his
face together   red hair defining chaos   legs bowed as if
condemned to straddle an invisible barrel   a sailor   a true
man of the sea   knife   marlinspike   boatswains pipe   like
the ancient mariner i read about in kelly's book   with a tale
to tell if he could just spit it out

the wind blows the heat from the ship

a cloud covers the face of the sun for a moment   and then
moves on

the sea rises like the hump of a whale

and life grinds away under my feet tumbling and rolling
pushing the owasso south

two

i make my way down to the hole   chief wheeler sits on a
stool in a corner   cap resting on his knees   biting the back
of his hand   gnawing at his knuckles

he catches my eye

```
        rat             rat      i
```

he shakes his head

```
    i didn't know rat        really
    i know you tried to tell me       but i
    didn't know it was that bad
```

he stares at me   looking for forgiveness   wanting to be told
it's okay   and he wants it from me

```
    if i had known this was gonna happen
    you know i would've done something rat
```

why me chief   go be forgiven by the captain or the other

chiefs   or go see the chaplain   that's his job isn't it
forgive and give hope   forgive and give strength   but why
me chief   because i know you ignored it   you stuck your
head in your little green book   didn't look up for even a
moment   you knew it all   knew exactly how the world
worked   were positive you had it all figured out chief   and
then it all came down   and now you're sorry   and you can't
stand it

he sits there   hunched over   looking sad   looking pathetic
  but i still want to push my fist into his face   knock his head
against the bulkhead   until he really feels sorry   really
regrets the past

but i can't

```
    forget it chief        it's over       i
    mean      who knows                 these
    things get going and then no one can stop
    em

    maybe rat      maybe you're right
```

he places his hat on his head

```
    maybe rat
```

he gets off the stool   lays a hand on my shoulder   then
disappears up the ladder   leaving me alone in the hole

alone with his little green book that sits on the work
bench   i walk over and pick it up   hold it in my
hand   run my thumb across the cover   i think about
flipping through the pages   find out what makes it so
important   see what the big deal is   but i don't
want to know   maybe i'm afraid it'll have
something in it that'll make me feel different   maybe sorry
for the chief   and sorry for ericson   and not so sorry for
holmes   or maybe there's stuff in it about me   stuff i
don't want to know   stuff that's the truth   so i hold it in
my hand   look at it   i touch the warped cover   the
broken spine   the folded ends of the pages   it just doesn't
feel right   doesn't belong here   so i carry it up the ladder
and outside to the wind and the waves   and toss it
overboard   where it pulls away as if snatched by an
invisible line

the owasso rocks in the growing sea   sways from port to
starboard to port to starboard   rolling to the rhythm of the
waves   the rhythm of life

i climb down to the snipes' quarters   mcgregor's rack is
around here somewhere   he's probably sleeping   thought
i'd stop by anyway   apologize for having to bug him that
time   still feeling bad about putting him on the spot   i walk
around a corner   there's a bunch of guys standing there   i'm
pretty sure they're near mcgregor's rack   it seems to be some
sort of meeting   people talking   but the voices are
hushed   almost whispers   i hesitate   i don't want to
interrupt   so i stand there for a second   just waiting
i decide i'll talk to mcgregor later but someone turns around
and sees me   surprised   off guard   a kid caught
doing something wrong   or being somewhere he shouldn't be
the guy leans into the group and speaks and then turns back
to me

    hey rat   what's up man

everyone's looking at me now   like one of those foreign
movies where people turn and stare   frozen   like the
picture's stopped running   it's comical   but i feel like i've
done something wrong   invaded a secret place   i don't
know what to say for a moment   think maybe i should make a
lie up   but i'm not quick enough for that   whatever i
come up with will sound stupid   and anyway i haven't
done anything wrong   but i can't help stammering a little
somewhere between speaking and thinking

     i   i just came down to see mcgregor

a head pops up from the middle of the crowd   mcgregor
looks over at me   he gives a little wave   shit   this is all
wrong   everything's out of sync   i feel guilty about
something i haven't done   and now mcgregor's looking at
me weird and waving and not acting like himself

     hey rat

     hey mcgregor   sorry man   didn't
     mean to bust up your meeting   just
     wanted to say i was sorry about bugging
     you that time in the engine room

     no problem rat   i know it wasn't
     you   you didn't wanna do it
     forget it rat   you need somethin'
     else

```
no mcgregor      thanks

okay rat
```

i make my way down to the pit   still feeling like i've been
somewhere i shouldn't have been

```
                              four
```

kelly leans against his rack   in his underwear   glasses
pushed up on his face   staring down at the deck   running his
bare foot over a spot   like he's removing a blemish from the
ship   i lean on an elbow and look at him from my rack
holding a pillow to my chest   my feet tucked just under the
folded blanket   gomez sits on a small stool he's taken from
the hole   working his magic fingers on the net or whatever it
is he's making   eyes blinking   like there's a beat going on in
his head   some catchy tune that his body works to

kelly looks up at me

```
     strange not havin' ericson and holmes
     around
```

he pushes his glasses up on his nose

```
     i nevah had to bury anyone befaw        you
     rat
```

```
     no     not like that        not that kind of
     hands on stuff
```

robert a kamarowski

```
how 'bout you gomez


no       an i don won to do it agen
eether       i feel strange when i do
eet         like       i don know       like
i responseeble       or like i the one
sendeen him eento the nex worl
```

he stops his hands and looks at kelly   then me   then goes
back to his knots   trying to tie up his head as well as his
fingers

kelly looks down and rubs at the deck again

```
    strange stuff        strange
```

he climbs in his rack and opens a book   let the real world
drift for a while   get lost in a story that's set far away from
the ocean and dumping bodies into the sea

i close the tiny light behind me   i was hoping the owasso
would rock me to sleep   roll me like a child in her arms   but
she's riding rougher all the time   shifting to one side or the
other   occasionally catching a wave just right   or just
wrong   then there's a powerful slap   enough to turn her
head but not enough to bruise   not yet   so I don't know if
i'll get the gentle sleep i hoped for   but i'll sleep

five

i'm being rocked   i think it's the ship   swinging from
side to side   but it's a hand   on my shoulder
shaking me now   a little harder than before   and there's a
voice   one i should recognize   one i should know

            rat   hey rat   c'mon man   we
            gotta get up   come on rat

            leblanc

            yeah   weather's gone to shit
            chief want's us to stow all the lines on
            deck   you and i gotta go forward and
            take care of the bow line   come on

            yeah yeah   ok leblanc

            you awake now

            i'm ok man   really

robert a kamarowski

i drop out of the rack   trying to shake the sleep from my
head   i grab my pants and make a stab at getting them
on   but i can't find the leg   so i hop around   until the
owasso shifts to port and i almost fall   so i sit on the deck and
hump my way into the pants   someone sits next to
me   kelly   and his voice is angry   which i'm not
used to

```
i can't believe this          nawt even one
decent nights sleep       aftah those hawt
nights lyin' awn deck
```

he pushes his foot into a boot

```
what about these cadet guys       what the
hell are they heah fowah anyway
takin' up space mostly
```

he laces up his boots and cleans his glasses

```
you okay now kelly
```

```
i guess      don't try and put me in a good
mood rat okay        ahm enjoyin' this
bitch session
```

```
you got it kelly
```

i lace up my other boot and follow him up the ladder

six

the wind moves across my face   the sea rises all
around   mounds of black with tops of foam like white
hair   the ship rolls to port   then to starboard

i walk toward the bow

the chief meets me under the bridge wing his black form
swaying in front of the rising sea

```
    good man rat           help leblanc with
    the bow line      then check everything out
    up forward       make sure there's nothing
    loose banging around
```

his voice is strange   full of life   not the dull sound of the
last few days or the weak whisper when we were in the
hole   he steps forward and slaps me on the shoulder like
we're good friends long lost buddies   a hatch opens to my
left throwing light into the night   i can see the chief's face
more clearly now eyes wide as if they're going to pop out of
his head   mouth in a wild grin   all teeth with the lips

pulled back   almost not a smile at all   and he has no
cap on   the thin hairs sticking wildly out in all directions
looking worse than rodgez   the hatch closes and the night
covers him again   but the look on his face is stuck in my
head

he slaps my shoulder one more time and leans his face in
close to me   his breath heavy and sour with alcohol

```
you're a good man rat        a good fucking
man            now go give leblanc a hand
oh        and hey rat    you know i can't
find my book    the little green one i
always carry around    i left it in the
hole and it's not there anymore        but
it doesn't matter    i don't care        in
fact i'm glad it's gone        you don't
know who took it do you        because if you
did i'd like to know so i could shake his
hand and thank him
```

he stands there   swaying as i look for words   try to find the
guts to tell him i tossed it over the side   but he doesn't wait
around   he just gives me a little salute and staggers aft
struggling against the rocking ship and the alcohol   and
maybe something else   there's more than booze in his head
he's not the same chief not the same man   the ship rolls to
port and his black form falls drunkenly against the
superstructure   like he wants to shoulder the bulkhead out
of the way   then the owasso rolls to starboard   and

pulls the chief's unsteady legs to the lifelines   where he holds
on and looks out over the growing hills of water   the wind
distorting his uniform   pressing it against one side of his
body and blowing it away from the other   he stands and
stares   then he raises a hand   like he's signaling to
someone   trying to get their attention   until he staggers
back to port as the owasso pulls him safely to her breasts

i turn and walk to the bow   needing some serious sea
legs   having to lean against the tipping of the ship   first
one way   then the other

a voice calls my name   hollow and distant   like it's coming
from the past

    `rat!`

i glance up at the bridge wing where mr templeton holds a
megaphone to his mouth with one hand and his hat on his
head with the other

    `rat!     have the bow lookout report to`
    `the bridge!`

    `yes sir!`

    `he's to come immediately to the bridge`
    `rat!`

    `yes sir!`

i wonder why he's even bothering with the cap   why he
doesn't just take it off and leave it inside   but as he lowers
the megaphone i can see the skull behind him   following his
every move   the old man

i lean against the wind   press myself into the rising
breeze   walk carefully across the moving deck as it shifts
from side to side

the lookout stands just in front of the five inch mount   a
cadet   his back to the gun   the barrel telescoping out over
him like the horn of a giant beast

i get his attention

```
        mr templeton wants you on the bridge now

        yes sir
```

i almost laugh   must be the weather   the rising sea and the
racing wind   him calling me sir

```
        don't make any pit stops      he wants you
        to report there right away
```

he says 'yes sir' one more time and moves carefully aft
happy to get away from the waves that are so close up
here   so close it seems i can reach out and place a hand on
them

equatorial rhythms

'bout time you made it up here ratman!

leblanc comes up to my side   we shout over the wind

i was wonderin' if you got up or not

i stopped and talked to the chief   and
mr templeton wanted the bow lookout to
report to the bridge

what the chief say

nothing of much use   you talk to him

a little   i got a whiff of his breath
and backed off so far we were in different
time zones   he rattled on and on 'bout
the weather and me bein' a good man

i guess we're all good men in his
condition

he better watch it   the old man catches
him shit faced like this and he'll wish
he'd never seen a boat

i think he wishes that now

what

```
never mind     you ready


yeah      all set      the hatch is open
i'll go down and you feed me the line


you want me in the hole        you're
senior leblanc


don't worry buddy      it's only blood
no ghosts down there
```

he smiles and climbs down   i feed the end of the bow line to
him   he draws it into the hole where the blood of holmes
and ericson dries to black   absorbed by the hawsers
maybe visible for years to come   i wonder if leblanc can feel
anything down there   a kind of presence   or memory

the end of the line goes into the hole i stuff my head down
the opening

```
that's it       you need any help


all set rat      just me and the ghosts


i'll get any loose gear that's out on deck


okay      yo hey rat


yeah man
```

equatorial rhythms

```
hang on baby    we're rockin' more and
more

i know leblanc    i feel it too
```

i walk from one side of the bow to the other   checking all
the equipment   looking for anything loose that may roll off
the ship   but there's nothing around except the immense
sea   huge mounds of black towering up to my head   like
strange animals peering over the lifelines   watching me
dance as i try to keep my balance   their voice a strange
whistling wind that rattles my shirt   and fingers my
face   and gathers strength

leblanc climbs up on deck   he secures the hatch to the
forward hole and gives me a wave and then moves aft

the bow of the owasso climbs up into the night   as if
climbing to the top of a mountain   there's a
pause   i hold my breath   like the moment at the very
top of a bridge   wondering if i'll make it to the other
side   then the ship plunges down as though dropped
from a great height   plummeting through the night
removing the deck from my feet   pulling my stomach up to
my throat straining at my hands that hold like death to the
lifeline   the bow drives into the sea sending wild white
foam into the air   to come raining down on the deck
running over me with sticky white fingers burning with salt

i move away from the bow   holding the lifeline   being
careful of each step   when the distant voice calls again from
the bridge wing   i see mr templeton   still holding onto his
hat

```
rat!        rat!      the chief!      get
the chief!
```

i stare at him   not knowing what he means   so he takes off
his hat and shoves it furiously at the bow of the ship

```
the chief rat!     the chief!       he's on
the bow!       get the chief!
```

i look forward   he must have gone on the other side of the
five inch mount   because i didn't see him   didn't even
know he was still on deck   but there he is   the chief
standing on the bow   not just forward not just on the
forecastle but actually at the bow of the ship   legs stitched
between the lifelines   leaning out over the ocean   arms
spread   shirt tail flying aft like some macabre figurehead

i turn to the bridge wing and signal that i see him

```
be careful rat           but see if you can
get to him       or at least get close
enough to where he can hear you        tell
him to come back          tell him to
report to the bridge immediately
```

```
immediately rat!      the captain wants to
see him
```

the hand of death grabs the megaphone   the white lips
press themselves to the tiny opening   and the deep flat voice
calls over the raging night

```
get him back here seaman ratkovitch!
get him back here now!
```

mr templeton stands to the side   one hand holding his
cap   the other resting on the side of the bridge wing   he
looks in my direction   checks the captain   and then yells
something down to me   causing the old man to turn around
and stare at him   but he yells one more time anyway   and i
think it's 'be careful'   but i'm not sure

i turn to the chief   his arms outstretched   head thrown
back   face toward heaven   shirt attached to his body by
only one arm now   like the tattered flag of some sinking
country   struggling to show its colors   struggling to survive

the owasso raises its bow

higher   and higher

robert a kamarowski

reaching for the murky ceiling overhead

with the chief's pale body guiding it upward

pointing the way

to the very edge of the universe

with the wind charging out of the night

ripping the shirt off the figurehead and sending it into the
black sea

and time freezing

equatorial rhythms

the earth not turning

the owasso stuck in mid air

and my breath caught deep in my chest

the chief kisses the sky   arms spread   naked chest pressed
to the wind   screaming howling   blowing words to the
invisible stars   when a hole is torn in the clouds letting the
moon's rays shine through a cone of pale light that touches
the chiefs tortured brain lighting the madness on his face for
a moment   and then returning to its cell of darkness

and the owasso begins its long descent

                down

                down

        toward the valley between mountainous waves

robert a kamarowski

and the water of extinction that awaits below

and the eerie silence of the wet walls of black

plunging us into the center of the ocean

i hold on to the lifeline with both hands   the owasso jerks
the deck from under my feet   attempts to toss my body off
its back   relieve itself of one more weight   i watch the
chief   the tormented head and the intoxicated soul   his cry
touches my ears   the bizarre screech of a foreign bird
licking my face with its condemned tongue

```
'freeeeeeeeeeeeeeeeeeeeeeeeeeeeee!
```

the owasso plunges into the ocean sending a cascade of spray
far into the air   followed by a torrent of black ocean and
the froth from a rabid sea that washes onto the chief
climbs to his waist   his chest   his neck his head and
finally swallows him twisting him around its salty tongue
until i can only see the tips of his fingers

equatorial rhythms

and then there's nothing

i clutch the lifeline as the spray is blown across the
deck   baptizing the owasso

we plunge deeper into the ocean   sucked farther into the
indifferent mouth

        i hold on

            and wait

                and wait

finally the bow of the owasso begins to lift slowly under the
great burden of the sea   pulling itself gallantly out of the
death grip   out of the jaws   as mounds of water pour off
its deck   turning into great rivers that seek the ocean below

        and the bow appears out of the sea

            without the weight of its figurehead

i look at the nose of the ship   at the empty horror

    man overboard!

i scream at the empty space where the chief wailed to the sea

    man overboard!

i scream at the bridge wing over my shoulder

    man overboard!

i scream at the black water below

    man overboard!

i look over the side of the ship   hoping for a sign of the
chief   praying for his head to bob to the surface

i hear mr templeton's megaphone voice call 'man overboard'
to the bridge   and the man overboard call sounds across the
ship and sailors come out on deck like animals from
hibernation balancing themselves out to the lifelines
searching the sea in all directions leaning into the rising
wind

the chief   trapped in the cold wet mouth of the raging sea
rising up and down   so alone

and then it seems unreal the words that come across the
ship   it hasn't been long enough   we haven't had time to
check every inch of the water   and we haven't come
about   haven't taken any of the normal man overboard
maneuvers   when the thick monotonous voice of death
wails into the night   'cancel man overboard'   'cancel man
overboard'

i look up at the bridge wing   at the bloodless face of mr
templeton as he stares down at me   one side of him lit by
the searchlight   the other side of him black   he turns and
moves back into the bridge   leaving only the old man on
the wing   to turn his death stare on me   until the
searchlight goes black

i gaze again at the ocean   and look for the chief one more
time   with the voice of a tired leathery old man rolling
through my head   sounding beaten empty lost   'help
me'   'help me'

chief wheeler

seven

i stare at my coffee   watching the liquid swirl   the rocking of
the ship creating patterns that change with each wave   first a
long narrow tail   then a fat stomach   paisley shapes   with
bits of powdered milk floating around like life buoys

kelly sits to my right speed sits across from me   both in
silence   both looking at the ocean art in their own coffee

mcgregor comes down the ladder and stands by our table
we all lean to port   like characters in some cartoon   leaning
one way   then the other

mcgregor looks at me   fiery hair and beard round pumpkin
face red cheeks   his head sitting on his massive frame like a
weird bowling ball placed on a human body   his legs are
wide apart   and his thick hands rest on the table

    you see 'im go over rat

everyone's been avoiding the question   but no one will leave

me alone until it comes out of my mouth   they need the
words that'll make it true   make it real

```
yeah          i saw him go over


you see 'im in the water


no        i looked          and then i
yelled man overboard three or four
times          and then the man overboard
alarm went out


and then what


what the fuck mcgregor!       just what
the fuck!


what happen rat!


everyone came out of the fucking ship
mcgregor!     everyone scrambled on deck
to look for the fucking chief mcgregor!
  he was over the side mcgregor!      he
was over! the! fucking! side! mcgregor!
 we looked for a while    maybe twenty
minutes          maybe two          maybe
not even    maybe fucking seconds
mcgregor!          and then the man
overboard was called off!
```

my body shakes like i have the chills

mcgregor lays a hand on my shoulder

```
    you're a good man rat           you did
    what you could
```

so it's real now   now that i've said it   now that he's heard it
from my mouth   he's satisfied and lumbers away to his
engines to pass the word   confirm the rumors

speed finishes his coffee and taps me on the shoulder

```
    youokayman
```

and he heads up the ladder

only kelly remains   by my side   not saying a word   just
sipping his coffee   leaving me to feel like shit all on my
own   which is what i want   what i need

he pulls out a book from his back pocket and pretends to read

i look at the side of his face   his glasses tipped down   the
eyes piercing one spot on the page   and i can't stand the
world as it is now i refuse to believe what's done is done
and i won't tolerate one more pat on the back for standing by
and watching someone swallowed by the sea   i need to

scream   to vomit out this feeling   but the voice that comes
out is low   a whisper   ready to break apart

```
next person calls me a good man i'm going
to beat the shit out of him
```

and i leave kelly staring at his book

eight

the bridge at night   always a magical place for me   the
windows looking out to sea the brass railing that arcs along
the bulkhead the polished helm   turning gyroscope
and the sweeping arm of the radar looking for some object
to strike and echo back to the screen   always searching
always on duty

tallski has the helm he's a third class quartermaster kind of
quiet keeps to himself   his eyes are fixed on the
gyroscope   trying to keep the ship on course   struggling
with the helm   fighting it   like a wrestling match between
man and machine and sea

mr templeton stares out a porthole   he hasn't looked at me
since i stepped on the bridge he just gazes out at the night
out at the ocean out at the chief's grave

        captain on the bridge

we snap to attention   at least as much as we can on the
pitching bridge   the old man enters   returns mr

templeton's salute   says 'at ease' and wraps his dark gaze
around mr templeton   then tallski   then me   holding
each of us for a moment reading us   like he's deciding
something   he walks to the helm and stares over tallski's
shoulder at the course we're on   he looks out of a porthole
and then back to the gyroscope as though lining us up with
some object no one else can see   he moves to the small
watch table and checks the log book   running his long bony
fingers along each page   silently mouthing the words

he looks up at the chronometer on the bulkhead

turns to mr templeton

> `i'll be in my cabin      mr o'connel is`
> `scheduled to relieve you      i want to`
> `see him before he takes command of the`
> `next watch`

he turns and sinks down the ladder   disappears into his
cabin

the owasso takes a sudden blow to the starboard side   the
deck shifts to port   mr templeton and i grab the hand
rail   tallski falls to one knee and loses his grip on the
helm   freeing it to spin like a roulette wheel   place your
bets   this one's a sure winner   tallski scrambles to his feet
and regains control of the ship   but the ocean's moved
around to our beam and tips us over to port as if pouring the
liquid out of a bottle

equatorial rhythms

```
sorry sir

that's alright tallski      y'all do the
bes you can
```

mr templeton sounds tired   his charleston drawl weary
and he looks older   not like a kid anymore   the kid with
the light beard   peach fuzz we'd always tell him   don't stick
your head out from a tree mr templeton or someone'll pick it
off your body   he looks sad   and his eyes have lost their
sparkle

the owasso pulls itself upright and continues to starboard
like a drunk overcompensating   drifting too far one way
then too far the other   i wish this rocking would shake the
life back into mr templeton   but he just holds on to the
brass rail and stares out at the raging sea   refusing to look at
me even when he speaks

```
ahm sorry 'bout the chief rat        ah
ah sounded the man overboard alarm        ah
did

i know mr templeton                hey
forget it    we both did what we could

he's just goan too far            too far
```

not really talking to me now   talking to himself or maybe
talking to the sea

nine

the bow of the owasso lifts to the sky   high over the
ocean   to the top of a liquid mountain capped with white
foam

then the pause

hang on men!

the deck is pulled from under my feet as if a trap door has
opened   and my stomach has a knot that rises to my throat

the sea reaches out and cups the bow in huge hands and
pulls it into its gaping mouth   sending a giant flare of white
spittle into the air   followed by the army of saliva that floods
onto the deck   tearing bits of flesh from the owasso as it
retreats back to the sea

mr templeton looks around

he uncaps the tube that runs up to the flying bridge

equatorial rhythms

```
wondal!     you okay!        wondal!
    wondal!
```

he puts his ear to the tube   waits   then calls again

```
lookout!    report immediately!
```

he listens to the silence

```
rat     go up on the flyin' bridge and make
sure the lookout's okay          he's a
cadet      tell him to get down here

yes sir

and be careful rat
```

i step out on the bridge wing   where the first gray light of
dawn touches the uneasy night   and where the wind is
wild   an out of control whip slashing through the air   the
waves rising and falling and turning white with rage as they
hurl themselves at the owasso

the changing sky drops a few giant pouches of rain   soft
bombs that explode into wet circles the size of a child's
palm   on the deck   on the bulkhead   on my face   i can
almost count them   until they become smaller   and drop
faster   and start to heave down on the earth like tiny
darts   slashes of gray   pouring down so fast they blend

into one giant body   sheets of liquid   caught up in the
hatred that's infected the wind and sea   pulling a dull wet
curtain over this massive black and gray

i climb slowly up the side of the bridge   making sure of each
step   making sure of each hand hold   until my eyes clear
the flying bridge and i can see cadet wondal lying on his
stomach   arms wrapped around a vent that sticks up from
the deck   vomit on his face vomit on the deck   washing
away with the pounding rain   his back rises and falls   and
his feet move a little like he's trying to crawl along the deck

i scramble over and wrap an arm around a pipe and grab
onto him with my free hand as we dip toward the sea

        wondal!   wondal!   hey man   can you
        hear me!

his head raises off the deck   bloodshot eyes looking at me
white lips trembling   it's harvey!   harvey the cadet
trying to be a regular guy   harvey the regular guy trying to
be a lookout on the flying bridge

        sick!   i'm sick!

        i know   hang on man!

we dip down to the sea   far over to the port side   beyond
the point i've ever been   maybe beyond the point the

owasso's ever been   so far over i can look straight down to
the ocean below   i hold tighter to harvey and tighter to the
pipe   until the owasso finally stops its fall   pauses
and starts to rise again   pulling itself up from one knee   a
fighter refusing to go down   rocking back onto its
feet   preparing for another assault

i scramble over to the tube so i can ask for help from the
bridge   before i open it i see mr templeton looking over the
side of the bridge wing   staring down to the deck below
where a group of sailors watch the body of an officer   lying
on his side face turned toward the sea   arms and legs in a
pattern of sleep a red line running from his head and
flowering out across the deck   one of the sailors moves
closer to the body   almost over it his huge back like a
wall   red hair plastered by rain   red beard sticking out from
his face   his foot pushes the body over onto its back

the old man's lips are curled back in a smile   like he's
enjoying death   as rain washes the blood from his
forehead

the owasso continues farther to starboard   losing its balance
again

i hold onto the tube and turn back to harvey

        hang on!   hang on one more time!

robert a kamarowski

he clings to the pipe   vomits   we dip to the sea

the owasso pauses again

then starts to right itself

harvey forces himself to his knees   reaches a hand out to me
as he struggles to his feet   takes a couple of weak steps my
way   and then a wave pounds the owasso   out of
rhythm with the other waves   shifting the deck violently to
port and slipping harvey's feet from beneath his body
throwing him backwards away from my grasp away from
the pipe that was his savior pulling his back against the
lifelines   where he teeters for a moment   with a look of
surprise   until the owasso heaves its bulk farther under him
and harvey's look shifts to terror all color drains from his face
hands scratch at the wind and rain   his body falls over the
lifelines and into the sea   without a word

harvey

robert a kamarowski

the owasso swings back to center   gathers its legs

i look over the side

mr templeton's gone from the bridge wing

the sailors aren't out on deck

and the old man's death grin no longer stares up at me

the captain

ten

mr templeton hangs on to the brass rail with both hands   his
eyes darting from the sea to tallski to me   restless   jittery
he licks his narrow lips   shifts from one foot to the other
runs a hand over the pale hairs on his face   he takes his hat
off and sets it on the watch table   looks at it a moment and
then puts it back on his head   adjusts it carefully   like he's
getting ready for inspection   trying to look his best   and
he starts talking again   nothing complete   just words
battered into the air

        never know!

he shifts his weight   stands on one leg for a second   then
moves to another porthole

        they'll understand!

he runs a hand over his beard

        no choice!   no choice!

equatorial rhythms

tallski and i look at each other

```
had to be done!      had to!         no
choice in the matter!        absolutely!
no choice!       it couldn't continue!
```

a broken stick of lightning runs from the low sky to the sea

and the crack of thunder that follows is deafening

```
ah didn't know!      not really!      not
really what they would do!
```

his tragic black eyes run from me to tallski   back to me
pleading for something

```
damn! damn! damn!
```

lightning plunges into the sea

thunder explodes from the sky

the owasso loses its voice   drops its deep rumble   so that
despite the wind and rain and thunder   all i hear is
silence

eleven

the foul weather gear's like being in a sauna   it's keeping the
rain off   but i'm melting inside   leblanc and speed and
kelly and gomez and i form an odd circle   holding on to
whatever we can   fighting the heaving deck   the
mountainous waves rolling the owasso over their backs

i talked to speed on the way here   so he knows where we
stand   he knows what i'm about to say

        get ready to abandon ship

everyone stares at me   waiting to be told it's a joke

speed takes a step forward

        no shit man   engines are out
        we're tossing like a cork   don't
        know how this shit's gonna go

leblanc waves a hand in the air   like he's swatting a fly

```
i know the fucking engines are out!
you mean we're not gettin' 'em back on
line!

the snipes don't know how long they'll be
down         maybe for good          they
just don't know
```

a flash of lightning strikes the sea   thunder rolls through my
bones   the frenzied wind continues its wild dance   and
the sea grows angrier   and the owasso struggles in the
middle of all this madness   unable to hold course   unable
to put the waves in a favorable position   unable to protect
herself

we're helpless

```
are we takin on wautah

not yet           but we have to get the
small boats ready      just in case
```

speed moves to the small boat   and the rest of us follow

i cut the lines that hold the boat cover down   letting the wind
sail it off into the sky like a huge kite   flying in zigzag
patterns   until it crashes against a wave and collapses like a
fallen bird

gomez climbs inside the boat   he works more or less with
one hand   the other holding on to the gunwale the
transom   anything that will secure him to the boat

kelly and i get the lines ready forward   speed and leblanc
aft   working against the rain and wind and the heaving ship

                    a wave broadsides us

                                a mountain of water surges onto the deck

kelly slips and falls   he slides to the edge of the ship   one
hand holds a lifeline   the other still clutches the boat line
and his foot hangs over the end of the deck   tempting the sea
he scrambles to his feet   face white   rain soaked glasses
twisted on his nose

another wave crashes against the owasso

my feet are pulled from under me   i fall through the rain
the deck pounds my knees and scrapes my hands and runs
its grit across my forehead   i hear the lines snap   a
block and tackle pulls apart as the stern of the small boat
crashes to the deck leaving gomez hanging on at the upper
end grabbing for a line above his head   he stares at the
crumbling boat   and another fucking wave unable to

hold back for a moment unable to give him time for one
more move   one more thought one more chance   water
surges over the deck   wet lips suck me back into the
lifelines   and sever the small boat from its cradle   drag it
toward the black throat of the sea sending pieces of boat
into the air ripping chunks of deck from the owasso
whipping pieces of cable around   dragging gomez into
the sea   with the screaming voice of kelly yelling
'no!no!no!' fighting the wind

gomez

   pain   bile   i crawl on all fours   blood drips from my
forehead   vomit burns my mouth and washes over my
hand   i reach the superstructure   kelly sits looking aft
watching leblanc hold his leg   as the blood runs between his
fingers   turning pink in the rain   speed hanging on to him
in an odd embrace

kelly and i struggle aft

```
        fucked up is leg man      maybe broke
        i'll take care of him                you get
        to the other side     see about the other
        small boat

        you want a hand speed!

        no time dammit!    no time!    get the other
        boat ready!
```

kelly and i stumble to the starboard side   where the small
boat sits in its cradle   undamaged   looking like a miracle
looking like escape

we untie the boat cover and set it free   check the lines
forward and aft   make sure everything is secured
   and all the time there's a vision of gomez in my head   the
scared look on his face as he disappears into the waves

speed's voice forces its way through the wind

```
gimme a hand!
```

leblanc looks like a phantom   drained of all blood   white
as hate   he struggles to sit up   speed and i prop him up
against the bulkhead while kelly takes the first aid kit from
the small boat and wraps a bandage around his leg covering
the lacerated skin   avoiding the bump that must be bone
pushing its way out

speed kneels in front of leblanc   his face close   like he
wants to whisper something

```
hafta tie you down man!      Keep you from
goin' over the side!

whatever you gotta do speed      whatever
you gotta do
                    speed!      speed!
```

equatorial rhythms

```
whoa    whoa    yeahman    whatsup
```

```
don't let me die here man      just don't
let me die here
```

his thick body sits on the deck   face white   thinking
whatever he's thinking

speed holds a line out to me

```
got this off the fantail     gotta tie him
down rat    make sure he don't roll
around
```

i tie one end of the rope around an eye in the
superstructure   speed runs his end around a vent sticking
out of the deck   he pulls the line tight across leblanc's
chest   then ties it off

```
okay man    you're not goin' anywhere now
```

but all leblanc can do is nod his head up and down   as
though it weighs a thousand pounds

thirteen

i finish tying off a line   pain in my head getting stronger
making me dizzy   nauseous   like i'm working in slow
motion   i stop and look over at leblanc   watch the ghostly
face roll from one shoulder to the other   occasionally lifting
up and then falling back down   floating in and out of
consciousness   maybe he's better off   maybe he's
beyond fear   beyond caring about abandoning ship   or
about sinking into the sea

a wave comes over the side   but it doesn't have the power of
before   so i'm able to hold myself to the deck

speed has the hood on his jacket thrown back   the rain isn't
pelting down now   and the wind isn't as angry

speed and kelly and i catch each other's eye   but no one's
saying anything   no one wants to jinx it   but we're all
silently praying for the truth to be the truth   and not
another lie

then from the bowels of the owasso comes thunder like i've
never heard

fourteen

the explosion comes from deep within the ship   far below
the water line   at the very heart of the owasso   where the
snipes have been trying to bring the engines back to
life   fighting fatigue and heat and the tossing of the deck
below their feet   then something goes wrong   something
gives way   someone turns the wrong valve   or trips and
stumbles against the wrong switch   the explosion comes
out the port side of the ship with the sound of ripping metal
and twisting pipes and expelling a black foul
breath   we're tossed off our feet   landing hard on the
deck   reaching for something to hold onto as the ship
shivers and tips to starboard   with the agonizing yell of
leblanc ripping through the air   but there's nothing we can
do for him   we're struggling to get back on our
feet   when from out of the air comes mr templeton's
voice 'ALL HANDS ABANDON SHIP!   ALL
HANDS ABANDON SHIP!   ALL HANDS' and is
silenced by another piercing blast   the ship jerks under
us   and we list a little more to starboard   reach a little
closer to the sea

speed raises himself to his feet and moves to the small boat

get the boat over!   do it!   now!

kelly and i follow behind   all done by habit   not
thinking   just getting it done   grabbing a line and
wrapping it around a drum and belaying the line to the
crucifix and swinging the boat out over the side and holding
it above the sea   the sea that's not wild and powerful
anymore   but large and rolling   hills of deep blue moving
past the owasso   we remove our foul weather gear
speed and kelly go for leblanc they half carry half drag him
to the edge of the deck that continues to tilt farther to
starboard   we stand leblanc up and put his arm around
speed's neck   kelly and i guide them into the small boat but
they end up falling awkwardly   thumping against the
bottom of the boat   speed rolls over and crawls to the
stern then waves us aboard   kelly and i look at each
other   should we look for more sailors   try to find
anyone else   a forward hatch opens and a sailor stumbles
out   face bloody   clothes torn   one arm blackened by
fire   and eyes of the damned   wide and yellow   bloody
lips open to bloody teeth and a screeching voice escapes

dead!   all fucking dead!

he looks up at the sky   and another explosion lifts him in
invisible arms and hurls his body far out to sea

the owasso dips farther to starboard   and speed yells at us

equatorial rhythms

wegottatogooooo!   wegottagonow!

we drop the small boat into the water   it splashes and rocks
and screams with leblanc's voice   then kelly climbs down
the rope ladder first   moves aft sits next to speed and waves
me aboard   i drop down the ladder   one rung at a
time   my feet touch the deck   i climb over leblanc and
sit forward   speed starts the engine   we untie lines and
then we're free of the owasso   alone in the giant
sea   moving carefully away from the ship   and
rodgez comes out of the hole like an animal from its
lair   we yell for him   he spots us   hesitates a
moment   takes three giant strides and leaps into the air
and is a strange bird with hat flying off and arms reaching
forward and his fingers touch the gunwale and his face
smashes into the hull and i reach into the water and grab
onto the short wild hairs and pull until my balls crawl up
inside my stomach and kelly comes over to help and i fall
back against the deck and look in my hand at the strands of
red that lay against my skin like veins that have popped out
of the muscles with the bloody ends topped with skin and an
explosion and a warm blast of air across my face and pushes
the small boat sideways across the ocean and blows a chunk
of the owasso into the sky and sends a monstrous tongue of
fire high overhead surrounded by smoke that's thick and
black

the stern of owasso slips back into the sea   swallowing
ocean   growing heavier and heavier   dragging down

the bridge wing   and the bridge   until all that's left
above water is the bow of the ship   reaching its strange
lips into the sky and begging for one more gasp of air   then
falling into the black of the sea

rodgez

the owasso

sun

one

we circle the spot where the owasso went down   everyone
expecting it to surface like a submarine   everyone except
leblanc   his eyes remain closed   his breathing unsteady
making a wheezing sound   and every once in a while a
pinkish bubble comes out of his mouth and sits on his lips
until the next weak breath breaks it apart

there's debris scattered everywhere   life jackets   bits of
clothing   a can of shaving cream   some boots   all
inside a huge oil slick that clings to the sea like a blanket
riding up and down the gentle waves

and the bodies

there's not that many   at least not that i can see   maybe
nine or ten   floating face down   blood   burns   maybe
nothing   but they're all dead   i feel dark   tingle from
head to toe   and i wonder what they went through
wonder if they had a moment to think of something or

someone   were they scared   or were the last few
moments calm   peaceful   accepting

the clouds break apart   the sun paints the oil slick purple
and blue and green and rains its heat down on my head

```
we're gonna have to protect ourselves
from the sun
```

i feel guilty thinking about the sun   thinking about myself
maybe the rest of my life should be spent grieving for my
dead shipmates   but i dread the sun and its heavy light
and fear the scorching fingers that can penetrate my brain

```
you'rerightman      wegottadosomethin'
```

speed moves the boat up and down the oil slick   weaving
around the debris   the wreckage that was the owasso
and the bodies that were her crew   we look for something
large enough to protect us from the sun   a tarp   a piece of
canvas to build an awning   anything to provide some
shade but there's nothing   speed puts the boat into
idle   and we drift up to a body   and i hold my breath as i
cut the shirt from it   careful not to roll the face over
careful not to look into the eyes   careful not to see if
something's been eating at it already   the shirt's open in
front   so all i have to do is cut it away from the arms   and
toss it on deck

equatorial rhythms

kelly cuts away the next shirt

and i take the one after that

      we drift toward a fourth   and there's a fin
slicing through the water   make that two
three   six or seven now   smooth and strong
submerged missiles

one passes about ten feet from the boat

     `they're all around us speed`   `we`
     `gotta get outta here man`

but the sharks aren't paying attention to us   they're more
interested in the smell of blood   in finding food
surviving

the water breaks into a yellow and pink froth   it boils with
the wild thrashing   painting the sea red

speed moves us out of the ring of death

and kelly cries not real loud not like on tv or at the

movies   you wouldn't even know it except for the shaking
of his shoulders   and the look of grief on his face

i turn away   keep my eyes straight ahead   look out over the
endless blue sea   and try to lose the memory of the bodies
floating   and the feeding

two

kelly's taken over the steering

speed's hurt   he holds his ribs and occasionally spits blood
over the side   said he injured himself falling into the boat
with leblanc   didn't even notice   adrenaline   or
maybe he just didn't want to say anything   anyway he
looks bad   slumped down in the boat wincing in pain once
in a while

leblanc hardly moves   his breathing's still uneven   he'll
gasp for air   and then he'll stop   not even breathe at all
as if he's forgotten how   a few seconds will pass   and he'll
start again   making little rapid sucking noises   his chest
still sounding wet   we've made him as comfortable as we
can   but there's not a lot we can do   nothing's on the boat
no food   no water   not even extra fuel   i can keep
from thinking about it   but once in a while my head fills
with fear   making me feel helpless   hopeless

kelly's all right since he had that little crying spell   watching
us pull away from the bodies got to him   but since he took

over the steering he's been fine   checking the tiny compass
once in a while   and scanning the ocean in front of us

i wrap a shirt around leblanc's head   no twitch   no
word   i don't think he knows what's going on   i don't think
he even knows where he is

speed spits more blood over the side then slides back to the
bottom of the boat   his face contorted with pain   his arms
wrapped around his ribs

and the lifeboat continues steadily west

three

the sun lifts its eyes over the horizon   casting a crimson light
into clouds that have lost their way and ended up at the
equator   and the sea reflects the sky   looking as
though someone dyed it red   or bled into it   it looks like
the first day of the earth   after all the explosions formed
mountains and hills and plains and rivers and oceans   the
very first day of calm in the world   with the ocean flat as
iron   and the sun ablaze   and the windless air searching
for its voice

the choking engine cuts through the sea   its sound cracks
the sky as it pushes the boat forward   and leaves a wake that
disturbs the dull plane of the sea

i feel everything else is gone   vanished   there's no land
no people   no ships or boats or airplanes or cars   just
the four of us   in search of something that's no longer there
moving toward a memory

four

silence   black   black silence   we've run out of
fuel   and just drift   not even drift   there's no
wind   no movement above or below

the stars are bright and deep   the moon a perfect cutout
glued up in the sky

leblanc sleeps   i think

speed groans   a wrong move twisting pain out from his ribs

kelly's voice travels through the night as though it hasn't
reached me on its own but carried by something invisible

> i wondah if the radiomin got a message out
> about owah status

> i don't know kelly

> should have sent something out somewhayah

equatorial rhythms

```
i don't know            you all right

hell no i'm not awhright     in the middle
of tha ocean not knowin if someone's out
lookin' faw us aw not
```

he sighs and i see his head turn

```
should be able to finish my book when the
sun comes up
```

i laugh

```
you have a book

two        had em stuck in my back
pawcket        they're on the deck now
drying out
```

i see his dark form look out over the sea   into the night
looking for something that probably isn't there anymore

five

floating bodies   lifting themselves up from the water   the
backs of their heads charred and hairless   hundreds
thousands   ripped clothes hanging off their
bodies   the water clinging to their dead skin   they move
through the sea   as though standing on something below
that pulls them toward me   the dead skin black and raw   as
they get closer   and closer   until the nearest one begins
to turn around   and i don't want to see his face   i don't
want to see who it is   i don't want to see what he looks
like   because i think i know him   and because he
shouldn't look like this   then in one swift motion he rips
the shirt from his scorched back and forces it at me   and no
matter how i try to move away he's always right in front of
me   blocking my path   as his head continues to
turn   slowly   slowly   slowly

the sun   behind us   its rays already heating the air
already baking my head

i look around   everything is blue   the water   the
sky   what wouldn't i give to see green   what wouldn't i
give to see a tree

speed's looking bad   holding his ribs   still coughing up
blood

kelly and i move awkwardly around the boat   trying not to
tip it over   trying not to fall in   and trying not to
make speed too uncomfortable   our movement sends
ripples out into the sea   strange tiny waves radiating out
from the boat   like it's the center of the universe   the
center of life   and the water is so clear   so clean   so
unspoiled

kelly balances himself in the boat   feet spread apart
bandanna across his nose and mouth   i know it's difficult to
do it the way it should be done   so i don't blame him for
using his knife   as he cuts away the shirt

i block the smell by holding my breath as long as i can
finally letting it out   then gulping air and holding it again

we tip the body forward   and the boat lists dangerously far
to port   right to the lip of the water   we each grab a
handful of pants and then lift for all we're worth   and
dump the body over the side   the boat swings like a
hammock until it regains equilibrium   kelly and i paddle
with our hands to move the boat to another spot   before
the feeding begins

leblanc

seven

thirst   it's worse than being hot   worse than being
hungry   i'd take a hundred more days of sun for one glass of
water   just one   tall and cool   with drops of moisture
running down its side

i keep my head under a shirt   a shirt from a dead
shipmate   a dead shirt   draped over my head   my
forehead rests against my arm   i stare down at the bottom
of the boat   at least when i have my eyes open
which isn't often   look at what   same footprint
same drop of oil   same nick in the fiberglass   same
pebbles of non-skid painted onto the deck

i wish i could do something   stand for a minute   walk
around do some pushups   talk a little to kelly and speed
anything   but the sun is scratching my back and head
right through the clothes   and i'm so dry   this thirst
unbelievable   my throat's like a hot road   and my
tongue feels so big   like its growing and won't fit in my
mouth soon

speed's not doing too good   we tried to make him
comfortable after dumping leblanc over the side
dumping leblanc   easy to say   took out the garbage
washed my car   ate dinner   dumped leblanc over the side
paddled away   and then waited for the inevitable shark
feast   we made speed as comfortable as we could
moved his legs around and fixed a shirt around his ribs and
talked to him a little   but he didn't really want to talk   but
we kept talking anyway   more for us than him   wanting to
hear other voices   make believe everything's okay for a
while   i watched the sweat running down his skin   like a
clear liquid running over black wood   highlighting its grain
magnifying its design   his red eyes opened and stared
without blinking right at me   like they were accusing me
of knowing something   something i'm not telling him

strange   but i can't believe kelly's not going to get out of
here   he's got to be picked up   the world can't go on without
him   so i guess if i stick by his side i'm okay

robert a kamarowski

speed moans   a wet cough follows   he's probably spitting
something up again   i just can't seem to move right
now   in a minute i'll check him   as soon as i catch
my breath   and get the sun off my back

```
eight
```

the sun   piercing through thick lifeless air
    heavy   wet   got to get to speed   meant to
do that a while ago   has it been minutes or hours or days
    i haven't heard him in a while   i'll wait a little longer
 until the sun isn't so brutal

        water

                                just a little

        to wet my lips

nine

ohyeah!   they'rehere!   they'reherenow!

speed's voice   everything was so quiet
        and without the sun i could actually sleep
    but now speed wants to talk   or yell is more like it

yes!yes!yes! they'rehere!

he's sitting up   lit by the moon   with a look on his
face   like he's discovered something

can'tyouseethemmen!
can'tyouseewhatitallmeans!
they'vecome!   togetus!

i want to tell him no one's here yet   but my mouth is so dry
and the air so heavy   i don't think he's going to listen to
me

they'rehere!   they'vecome!

speed struggles to his feet   powerful body outlined
against the night   black against black against black   one
arm raised   the other holding his damaged ribs

     `justoverthere!`   `can'tyouseemen!`

     `you bettah lie down speed`

     `i'monmyway!`   `andsoaretherestayah!`
     `we'reallonourway!`

     `speed!`   `get down man`   `get down`

     `i'llbethefirst!`   `i'mchosen!`
     `i'mtheone!`   `theone!`

and speed hurls his body over the side

kelly and i move to the edge of the lifeboat   look out over
the ocean   call to speed   send his name into the night
over and over   but our words are weak   and die
as speed's voice explodes into the night   'i'monmyway!'
'i'monmyway!'   and the sea turns silver where he churns
the water with his erratic swimming   one arm clutching his
ribs   the other moving him through the ocean toward
someplace in his head

     `we gotta get him kelly`

robert a kamarowski

`i can't go out theah rat`

the thought of jumping into the sea terrifies me
black   bottomless   maybe
something's hovering just below the surface   waiting
for me   maybe all this has been a trap just to pull me
into the ocean and smother the life out of me

`rat!    rat!    listen!`

nothing   no splashing water   no crazed
voice   no wind
           no waves

                no more

speed

ten

endless blue sky   white sun   i don't want
to see it anymore   my head's covered
looking at the same spot on deck   the
same piece of non-skid   the same spot of oil

thirst   nothing else matters
only water   a cold glass of
water   i don't even want food
it makes me sick to think about food

tongue   growing   can feel it
expanding   maybe i'll say something to
kelly   make sure i can still talk
   just a few words   ask how he's doing
what's the weather for today   yeah   get him to
laugh a little   or talk to him about sports
     ask him how much longer yaz will play   what
records he'll break   maybe he's not just staring
at the same piece of deck under the shirts on his head
        maybe he's fallen asleep   maybe i
have too   and i'm dreaming all this

equatorial rhythms

i'll wake up in a few hours and the sun will be gone
just the silence of the night
        maybe i'm dead

    wherever i'm going is a longer journey than i thought

    a long long road   taking forever

        maybe my father's there   i'm being held up
because he wants to get ready
        wants to figure out what he'll say to me
wants to look his best

        maybe they had to send for him

robert a kamarowski

they

eleven

mom!

mom!

don't forget about dad!

do what you gotta do

do whatever you want

but don't forget about dad

okay

just don't forget

twelve

water water everywhere and not a drop to drink

water water everywhere and not a drop to drink

water water everywhere and not a drop to drink

equatorial rhythms

water water everywhere and not a drop to drink

water water everywhere

and not a drop to

robert a kamarowski

drink

water

equatorial rhythms

water

everywhere

robert a kamarowski

and

equatorial rhythms

not

a   drop

robert a kamarowski

to drink

```
                    thirteen
```

strange sound   getting closer

can't feel my tongue   i think my mouth is open

         but i can't feel my tongue

                         touch it

                   it's huge

like sandpaper   cheeks swollen

          i can't push my tongue back in my mouth
it's going to take over my whole body

     pull up my eyelids   try like hell to lift them
think i have them open now
                    but everything's blurry

                              and it hurts

robert a kamarowski

i don't care

i don't care

i don't fucking care

lift my head   just a little

the sound is closer   and there's a
weird shape over me now
an insect
a giant insect
getting larger
coming right at me
massive
too big

crazy wings

a whirring noise

equatorial rhythms

over and over and over and over

churning the water

blowing the shirt off my head

its voice is weird

metallic

barely reaching my ears

oh fuck

i've lost it

i've fucking lost it man!

forgive me mom

forgive me for not forgiving you

the insect

the metal voice

robert a kamarowski

i can understand it!

i can understand it!

equatorial rhythms

i can understand it!

the end

If you enjoyed this book, please check out
my other seafaring adventure,
wind dancing.

Get your copy here
books2read.com/equatorialrhythms

www.ingramcontent.com/pod-product-compliance
Lightning Source LLC
Chambersburg PA
CBHW051945220626
47052CB00004B/797